"That child and I have the power to repel the 'evil' that will envelop this world someday. Right now, we have to make sure this power remains safe."

THE DEVIL IS A PART-TIMER!

SATOSHI WAGAHARA

ILLUSTRATED BY ■ 029 (ONIKU)

11

YEN ON

NEW YORK

THE DEVIL IS A PART-TIMER!, Volume 11
SATOSHI WAGAHARA, ILLUSTRATION BY 029 (ONIKU)

Translation by Kevin Gifford
Cover art by 029 (oniku)

HATARAKU MAOUSAMA!, Volume 11
© SATOSHI WAGAHARA 2014
First published in Japan in 2014 by KADOKAWA CORPORATION, Tokyo.
English translation rights arranged with KADOKAWA CORPORATION,
Tokyo, through Tuttle-Mori Agency, Inc., Tokyo.

English translation © 2018 by Yen Press, LLC

Yen On
1290 Avenue of the Americas
New York, NY 10104

Visit us at yenpress.com
facebook.com/yenpress
twitter.com/yenpress
yenpress.tumblr.com
instagram.com/yenpress

First Yen On Edition: August 2018

Yen On is an imprint of Yen Press, LLC.
The Yen On name and logo are trademarks of Yen Press, LLC.

Library of Congress Cataloging-in-Publication Data
Names: Wagahara, Satoshi. | 029 (Light novel illustrator)
  illustrator. | Gifford, Kevin, translator.
Title: The devil is a part-timer! / Satoshi Wagahara ;
  illustration by 029 (oniku) : translation by Kevin Gifford.
Other titles: Hataraku Maousama! English
Description: First Yen On edition. | New York, NY :
  Yen On, 2015–

Identifiers: LCCN 2015028390 |
  ISBN 9780316383127 (v. 1 : pbk.) |
  ISBN 9780316385015 (v. 2 : pbk.) |
  ISBN 9780316385022 (v. 3 : pbk.) |
  ISBN 9780316385039 (v. 4 : pbk.) |
  ISBN 9780316385046 (v. 5 : pbk.) |
  ISBN 9780316385060 (v. 6 : pbk.) |
  ISBN 9780316469364 (v. 7 : pbk.) |
  ISBN 9780316473910 (v. 8 : pbk.) |
  ISBN 9780316474184 (v. 9 : pbk.) |
  ISBN 9780316474207 (v. 10 : pbk.) |
  ISBN 9780316474238 (v. 11 : pbk.)
Subjects: CYAC: Fantasy.
Classification: LCC PZ7.1.W34 Ha 2015 | DDC
  [Fic]—dc23
LC record available at
http://lccn.loc.gov/2015028390

ISBNs: 978-0-316-47423-8 (paperback)
  978-0-316-47424-5 (ebook)

1 3 5 7 9 10 8 6 4 2

LSC-C

Printed in the United States of America

PROLOGUE

On the night that Maou, Suzuno, and Acieth set off through the Gates of Hell in Ueno-Onshi Park for Ente Isla, Chiho gingerly looked up at the figure standing to the side, too preoccupied to worry much about Urushihara now that the screaming siren of the ambulance that took him away was no longer audible.

That figure was Miki Shiba, landlord of Villa Rosa Sasazuka and a woman that Maou and Ashiya seemed to morbidly fear, and certainly, seeing her in person like this made Chiho realize the sheer impressive force that her body projected. Not the literal, special kind of overwhelming power that angels and demons seemed to bandy around her lately, though. To Chiho, she was just a middle-aged woman who weighed a fair bit and preferred to advertise it with excessively loud clothing.

If there was anything odd about this meeting, it was that she and Shiba were having their first encounter alone in the apartment. Just a moment ago, Chiho was having the secrets of the world, so to speak, unveiled to her by Amane Ohguro, Shiba's niece. Amane seemed to know about Maou's true nature, as well as that of the demons from Ente Isla, and the Sephirah, and the life-giving trees that powered entire worlds. Maou and Suzuno had just gone off to rescue Ashiya, Emi, and Alas Ramus, and Chiho felt obligated to gather more intel while they were gone. Miki interrupted that—and then Urushihara, trying to eavesdrop on them, fell unconscious and ended the interrogation for good.

The landlord's sudden appearance clearly made Amane panic, and Urushihara was nonresponsive in Devil's Castle. The landlord wound up making Amane summon an ambulance, and before very long, both Amane and Urushihara were gone. So, at around two in the morning, Chiho found herself alone with this woman.

"Now, about Amane—"

"Y-yes?!" Chiho asked, frazzled. The woman didn't bother turning to her.

"Amane's always taken kind of an easygoing approach to things, I know. She wasn't rude to you at all, was she?"

"Um… Rude how, do you mean…?"

"I mean, did she give you any incorrect information, as the off-spring of a Sephirah?"

"Oh…" This threw Chiho. She recalled Amane's own words: "Miki Shiba's another Sephirah child."

"I, umm…" the girl stammered.

Which meant that, if anything, the woman in front of her lay at the very core of the truth Chiho wanted to learn, even beyond Amane. She opened her mouth, attempting to continue where she had left off a moment ago, but was stopped.

"Chiho Sasaki."

The name stopped Chiho cold. Not because Shiba couldn't have known the name, this being their first encounter; no, it was something else. Chiho swallowed, her very soul submitting.

The moment her name was invoked, every fiber of Chiho's consciousness fell to its knees before this insurmountable force. It brought her back to her younger years, when her mother yelled at her for committing some forbidden act. Her heart commanded it to her—the figure in front of her must not be defied.

"Allow me to make one thing clear: You knowing the truth will not allow you to change a single aspect of it. You realize that, and yet you still want to know everything?"

"…I…"

"You were born on this world, without any special sort of ability, and that is exactly what makes you special. It seems you are unaware of the meaning behind the slight amount of holy force housed within your body. Knowing everything may very well cause your heart to break, leaving you unable to bear your powerlessness any longer. Yet you still wish to know?"

She didn't understand the question. Of course she didn't. If she did even try to figure out the meaning of what Miki had just said, then of course she wouldn't comprehend the question either. "Even…"

"Yes?"

"Even if knowing makes me curse my powerlessness, or gets me scared and I regret it later…"

She willed her soul to get up off its knees. There was no pulling back. She didn't have the force, the knowledge, even the life required to fight in unison with them—she knew how little she was capable of. But doing what little she could was the hill she had to die on. If what she learned made her flee the scene and simply become a passive observer, she'd no longer be able to stand next to them all.

"I don't want to run away from knowing. If I do, I feel like it'll all be over."

"…"

"Even if that new knowledge doesn't enable me to do anything myself…the me who understands that situation will be born. So I…"

Her wispy body fought back the stillness of the night, and the overwhelming pressure placed upon her soul.

"I believe that, if I know everything, someone with the power to care for me can use that. As a tool. To fight and change all of this!"

At that moment, Chiho could feel the force attempting to bind down her heart loosen a little. Shiba looked down at her admiringly. "…My," she said, clutching at the gold chain on her purse.

"I'm sorry if this is brazen of me. I know I'm powerless, and I'm not saying this out of some noble creed or what have you. It's just…" Chiho looked up toward Villa Rosa. "I want to stay friends with the people I love. That's the only reason why I'm here."

"There are few, indeed, who can fight for the sake of such motivations. I think I'm starting to see why She put her eyes upon you."

"...Oh?"

The force on Chiho's heart subsided as Shiba extended a hand toward her.

"I'd like you to stay at my home tonight. I could hardly ask you to venture home by yourself this late, and it'd be rude of us to enter a tenant's apartment without permission."

"A-all right..."

She had a point. They couldn't just invite themselves into Maou's Room 201, and Amane, currently house-sitting for Room 202, was in the ambulance.

Chiho meekly agreed to the offer and followed her into the Western-style house next to Villa Rosa. It boasted a large yard area and a house about three times that of Chiho's own—by inner-city standards, it was a stately manor. Going through an entryway that would've looked at home in a prime-time soap opera, she made her way to an elegant, refined-looking parlor.

"I know it's late," Shiba said as she motioned for her to sit on a sofa decorated with embroidered silk, "but I have a question or two for you as well, if that's all right with you?"

She provided some fresh, steaming tea for the nervous teenager. One mouthful of the soft, sweet, fragrant drink ever-so-slightly took the load off the young woman's shoulders.

"Now, Amane might have told you already, but on this world of Earth, there used to be something known as the 'Tree of Life.' This tree bore a jewel—a Sephirah—that forms the structure of a world; it was a keystone in creating human life."

"O-okay..."

Chiho suddenly realized that she'd left her pen and notebook in Suzuno's room.

"Oh, you can write this down if you like," Shiba said, providing paper, a feather pen, and a jar of ink from nowhere in particular.

"Th-thank you."

Chiho began to write, struggling with these wholly unfamiliar instruments, but before she could even put a complete thought down, Shiba unleashed a bombshell.

"As a rule, all of the Sephirah are required to stay within the world they were born in."

Once she understood what this meant, Chiho instinctively tried to hide her right hand. It didn't escape Shiba's notice. Her eyes turned toward the Yesod fragment embedded in Chiho's ring.

"Lately, though, the Earth has been visited by Sephirah that, well, don't belong to it. I cannot feel them right now, but I very much doubt they have returned where they came from, now have they?"

That was the question. Which Sephirah was Earth's?

"The Sephirah jewels hold the information needed to build worlds. Without them, the people who call that world home will slowly die out. They may survive for a short period, but the Sephirah still needs to go back to its world. As soon as possible."

As far as Chiho knew, this encompassed three people. One: Erone, a boy being dragged around by a demon. Two: Acieth Alla, the girl being dragged around by Maou. And three: Alas Ramus. The "child" of Emi and Maou, and a child that held an irreplaceable position in Chiho's life.

THE DEVIL AND THE HERO HAVE A GRAND DISAGREEMENT

The bank account had been wrung completely dry.

The reason couldn't be simpler: She had used up all the money.

What on? Well, first, there was that new cell phone that didn't even belong to her. She had chosen a low-cost model, but she had to buy it outright instead of through a new contract, so even with an outdated brand, the monetary outlay was considerable.

Next, there was the clothing. She had procured several outfits, suited for a middle-aged adult male; and covering everything from undies to shoes, no matter how much you bargain-hunted, cost a certain amount to cover.

That, and the debt repayment. She was reasonably confident about her savings up to now, but the sheer extent of the debt was so completely beyond her imagination that it placed unexpected pressure on her plans.

All of this—coming due at the same time, no less—had drained her cash.

"Um," the voice of a man in the prime of his life said, beating against her eardrums, "shouldn't you have been planning your finances a little better?"

"Oh, so you think it's all right for me to owe him money forever?

I should just let that demon of a debt collector harangue me for the foreseeable future?"

"I-I'm not saying that..." The man chose his words carefully as he rebuked her. "If you have no job and not enough funding... I mean, there is no guarantee we'll have any income after next month. Couldn't we use my funds, or set up monthly payments or the like?"

"I don't like being in debt."

"Well, no, neither do I, but—"

"And if we go on for days and days without settling this, who knows what the interest is gonna look like?"

"But—"

"Plus, what I'm worried about right now is paying people back karmically, you know? For everything I've had to borrow from everyone. If I can't get that squared away by my own volition, I can't really move on."

The scene was the living room of a fairly fancy apartment. In the middle of it sat a dour-looking daughter and a harried-looking father, sitting across from each other around a table with a cutely patterned cloth on it. The harried father suddenly stood up, opening the curtain on the wall.

"Then how about this, Emilia?"

Normally he would have more of a stern presence in his dour daughter's life, but now his face bore a look of resignation as he gazed at the cityscape.

"Could we at least move to the Villa Rosa Sasazuka apartments? I know *they* live there, but you have good friends in Sasazuka too, don't you? Bell, and Sasaki, and..."

"..." The girl called Emilia let off a sigh soft enough for her father not to notice. "I told you, I can't leave here right away." She stood up and walked next to her father. "I mean, I know a lot of stuff has happened, but I like this place. I like this neighborhood. And I don't even have the money for moving expenses right now. I mean, the way it's worked out, there's only about a five-thousand-yen rent difference between here and there, and if I can live cheaply enough, I'll have my last month's salary before too long, but I can't do anything until then, all right?"

"…Ah."

"Thanks to everyone else, my 'enemy's' gonna be gone for a while. If I can find a job fast enough, I should be able to make it out of this."

The sound of his daughter's voice didn't indicate to the father that this was impossible, or empty bravado on her part. But his intuition told him that this wasn't her entire motivation. She had, he thought, some other reason to not want to leave here. But his daughter was grown now; she had overcome countless obstacles. He had neither the right nor the courage to wrest the true reason out of her.

"But what about you, Father? Do you think your new life…well, not 'new life' exactly, but do you think it's going okay in Sasazuka?"

"Well… Acieth is whining at me about how she can't see the stars at night as well as before."

"That's downtown for you." His daughter laughed, then lowered her voice. "But what about…you know? Think you have any clues yet?"

"No," her father replied gravely. "Nothing. There's nothing to go on right now, so…"

"All right. But you're sure about this?"

The daughter, Emilia Justina, turned toward her father, Nord Justina.

"You're sure that Laila…that my mother is here on Earth?"

"She…should be," came the wavering reply.

Emilia frowned at it. "I'm sorry. I'm not trying to attack you, but…"

"No, no. You can't help it."

Emilia—the former Hero known as Emi Yusa—looked down at the neighborhood of Eifukucho.

"But the fact that we have no idea what Laila wants, or what she's trying to accomplish, is really starting to worry me."

✳

The environment surrounding Emi Yusa's life had undergone a rapid flurry of epic changes over the past month.

Returning to Ente Isla to track down the whereabouts of her parents, Emi wound up caught in unexpected trouble, preventing her from returning to Japan when she had planned to. For a while, she was helpless at the hands of three different forces: Efzahan, the Eastern Island kingdom that declared war on the rest of the world; the Malebranche demons that formed the core of the so-called New Devil King's Army; and Olba Meiyer, who conspired with the heavens to make the other two players do his bidding.

Sadao Maou, the Devil King Satan, quickly realized that both Emi and Alas Ramus—the fragment of the world-bearing Yesod seed that Emi held within her—needed help. But as he twiddled his thumbs, his close associate Shirou Ashiya (aka the Great Demon General Alciel) and even Emi's father Nord Justina got caught in the conspiracy, forced to return to Ente Isla.

So together with his neighbor, Church cleric and (tentative) Great Demon General Suzuno Kamazuki, and the fellow Yesod-born Acieth Alla, Maou made a grand journey back to Ente Isla to rescue Ashiya, Alas Ramus—and Emi, the greatest present obstacle to his world-domination plans.

Olba and the heavens sought to use Alciel and the Malebranche to create a scenario where the Hero Emilia once again routed the Devil King's Army from the Eastern Island—a ruse that Ashiya quickly picked up on. He knew that the heavens—along with Gabriel, an archangel among their forces—had their eyes set upon other goals.

And as the battle unfolded across the Efzahan capital of Heavensky, it was ultimately Maou and Acieth who stole the show. While Maou rescued Emi and Ashiya from the field of battle, Suzuno rescued Emi's friend Emeralda from the unfair inquisition she was enduring.

This gave them the tools needed to keep anyone from further laying hands upon Emi. But it also made life harder for her. Olba had seized upon her weaknesses. She had yearned for Maou, the greatest nemesis of her life, to save her from him. And she had reunited with her father, a reunion she thought would never happen. It was good for her, perhaps, but it had robbed her of all motivation to remain a Hero.

The Hero Emilia Justina, the fighter fated to slay the Devil King Satan who threatened all of Ente Isla, was no more.

But just because her father was here and her hatred for Maou had slackened a little didn't mean that everything was all neatly wrapped up. Laila—Emi's mother and the woman behind nearly all the drama around Emi, Maou, and countless Ente Islans—was still missing, her motivations unclear. As were the motivations for Olba and the heavens to make Emi and Ashiya simulate the liberation of the Eastern Island all over again—that remained a mystery as well.

And what of the mysterious astronaut, the one working and conniving behind Gabriel, Camael, Raguel, and the other angels?

To Emi, who no longer had the quest to defeat a Devil King motivating her, this was too wide an ocean to swim, the currents too choppy and transitional to read.

✳

"I'm home, Mommy!" came a bright voice behind the troubled-looking Emi. She turned around, relaxing her expression a little. Nord joined her, a tad perplexed at his daughter.

"Hi, Alas Ramus. Where'd you get that balloon from?"

The young girl was carrying a yellow balloon—not a string attached to it, but the balloon itself, carefully, like a summer watermelon.

"They were passing them out at the station. Advertising for some new wireless net provider."

The reply did not come from Alas Ramus. It was Suzuno Kamazuki, who accompanied Nord to Emi's apartment as his bodyguard.

"Grampa! Balloon!"

"Ooh, it sure is," Nord replied, smiling awkwardly at the proud Alas Ramus.

The way the family structure around her worked, Alas Ramus was

Emi's daughter, if not by blood. Her "sister" Acieth Alla called Nord "Pop," but as long as Emi was "Mommy" to Alas Ramus, it only followed that Nord was a grandfather figure to her. Emi had long accepted the "Mommy" role, and watching Nord struggle at being called "Grampa" made her wince a little.

"Thanks, Bell. Did you behave, Alas Ramus?"

"Uh-huh!" the girl shouted.

"Indeed. She was a perfect child."

Nord always had security with him, just in case. He was going to stay in Room 101 of Villa Rosa Sasazuka tonight, but whenever he had to go out, Suzuno went with him. She certainly had the free time for it, although she had gone with Alas Ramus just now so that Emi and Nord could discuss their finances in peace.

"Ooh, but no tellin' 'bout the donut!"

"Oh, did you have a snack outside?"

"Ooh, no tellin'! It's a secret!"

"We had best explain to her what a 'secret' is," Suzuno said meekly at this bout of self-incrimination. "She ran up to the donut shop and refused to budge, so I spoiled her a little. I apologize."

"Oh, that's all right. I'll pay you back later. Did you say 'thank you' to your big sis here, Alas Ramus?"

"Uh-huh! But no tellin'!"

The child looked up at Suzuno and gave a mischievous smile, balloon still in hand. She knew she had shared an experience with her, but she just couldn't hide it from anyone else. It made the grown-ups in the room smile.

"Hopefully this will not ruin her appetite."

"Oh, it'll take more than a donut to do that."

"Very well," Suzuno nodded as she watched Emi and Nord. "So, have you worked things out?"

"Not quite," Nord began, pleadingly.

"It's not gonna be easy," Emi interrupted, "but I don't think we're out on the street yet."

"But, Emilia..."

Suzuno smiled at the display of family politics.

"I told you," Emi fired back, "this is my problem. And it'll be fine! Compared to everything before now, being jobless and in debt barely even qualifies as trouble."

"But..." Nord looked around, upset. "Bell, at least, I'm sure could..."

Suzuno shook her head. "If that is what Emilia wishes, it is not for me to intrude."

"Thanks, Bell."

"But..."

Emi smiled boldly at the lost-looking man.

"Now, Nord," Suzuno deflected, "we had best return to Sasazuka soon. Emilia has a guest coming, and we have plans of our own to handle."

"Er, yes..."

"Emilia, Alas Ramus, I will see both of you later."

"Sure. Thanks for watching over Father."

"Bye, Suzu-sis! Bye, Grampa!"

"Y-yes," Nord said as he filed out of the apartment. He gave the building several furtive glances back as they walked the short distance to Eifukucho station.

"Nord," Suzuno asked as she observed this, "are you worried about Emilia?"

"Hmm? Well, no, not at this point, but..."

"I am."

"Emilia's hardly a young child anymore, and... Hmm?"

The casual admission made the depressed father stop cold.

"I know how Emilia works. With all the debt she rang up the other day, I am sure she absolutely insists upon paying everything back by her own power, yes?"

"Exactly. I told her I could cover some of it myself, but..."

They passed through the Eifukucho station gate and stepped up on the platform to wait for a train.

"At far too young an age, Emilia was forced to bear far too heavy a burden," Suzuno stated. "Now that the burden has vanished, she is unable to find solace. Either she needs some powerful spark to divert her mind, or we will just have to wait for her to acclimate to her current situation."

"..." Nord nodded and looked down, face troubled once more. "And I am the one who placed that burden upon her..."

"I can absolutely ensure you that Emilia does not feel that way. If anything, her current irritation is aimed almost fully at Laila. You, meanwhile, are the embodiment of everything Emilia strove for while bearing that burden. And now that you have miraculously come back together, I am sure she wants no burden to be placed upon you."

"Well, I'll tell you, as her father, it makes me feel pathetic." His face remained turned down. "I hardly did anything for her as a parent in the first place..."

Tomorrow marked the official date of Nord's move from his temporary lodgings in Mitaka to Room 101 of Villa Rosa Sasazuka. Emi had strongly suggested he find anyplace besides that apartment, but he had steadfastly refused.

Given how they had just made an incredibly improbable reunion after several years, one would expect Emi to invite him to live together, in her apartment at Urban Heights Eifukucho. But reality made that less than advisable. Nord was too close to the core mysteries of the Yesod fragments, far more than anyone else involved, and he needed to be carefully protected. Villa Rosa was at least some distance from Emi's place. The idea of leaving Nord alone in her apartment while she went off to work concerned her, and he could hardly join her on the job.

So in the end, she decided that, for better or for worse, Villa Rosa was full of people who understood Nord's predicament and, in a pinch, could be counted on to help. There was also the fact that Emi's apartment certainly had the free space, but was set up for single living—a multigenerational family in the place led to assorted inconveniences.

All this also meant, however, that Nord could not provide day-to-day support for Emi, the daughter he had just met for the first time in six years. He suggested at least helping with her debt a little bit, but even that was turned down today, much to his chagrin.

Suzuno looked up at this chagrined father with mixed feelings of her own. His daughter was in a bind, and not only couldn't he do anything about it, but she actively refused his aid. The worry and disappointment were wholly understandable.

But to Suzuno, the situation didn't seem nearly as dire as it did on the surface. Her biggest creditor, after all, was none other than Sadao Maou. Maou, who took the kind of regained power he had when he attempted to conquer the world and used it to march right back to the MgRonald by Hatagaya rail station and catch up on his borrowed shifts. The Devil King Satan, back to his normal life, willing to accept repayment for the debt the Hero owed him in money—Japanese yen, no less. After all they had been through, worrying about this turn of events seemed pointless.

"Though certainly," she whispered as she recalled the day after Nord and Emi had reunited, "I think you could have handled it better, Devil King."

Not long after Emi and Nord returned from Ente Isla, Villa Rosa landlord Miki Shiba generously unlocked the door to Room 101 and let them use it for Nord's recuperation. Suzuno was there as well, to check up on his condition. She was not left alone for long.

"Hey, Emilia the Hero? I'm comin' in."

Sadao Maou, barging in from upstairs, expressed a sinister smile as he made his way inside.

"Ah... Maou..." came the recognizing whisper from Nord. Emi let him inside, still not sure how to deal with him.

"You know why I'm here, right, Emilia? Why I'm visiting? Huh?"

Emi raised an eyebrow. This wasn't how Maou normally spoke; it seemed far too contrived. "...What?" she ventured, fully aware of the kind of debt she owed him.

"Oh," he replied, "I just figured I'd like to get repaid sooner rather than later, is all." He took out a piece of ruled paper ripped out of a notebook and thrust it at her. It was filled with handwritten numbers. Emi, dubious, picked it up and gave it a quick look...then turned to Suzuno, face drained of color.

"What is *this*?" she barely managed.

Suzuno peeked at the paper. Titled INVOICE up top in ballpoint pen, the table of figures began with the cost of obtaining Maou's scooter license and continued on down, covering every expense Maou incurred for Emi's sake from the day she went missing in Ente Isla. It was Maou's way of demanding compensation for the yen he'd laid out toward getting Emi back to Earth.

Emi knew, regardless of past grudges, that she'd have to pay Maou back for all of this. But her shaky voice was all due to the number at the bottom.

"I know you're gonna have a few expenses going forward and you have to find a job and all, so I'm not gonna expect it all at once. But you're an old pro at life in Japan by now, yeah? You know they got a little something called 'interest' here?"

"That..."

"Devil King, this is simply too much," Suzuno winced. Maou paid the reaction no mind.

"Ohhh? I'm sorry, do we have a complaint with this? Because this is a lowball estimate, let me tell you. I'm a fair Devil King, so I've taken off everything that was mostly my own fault. This is what's left."

The grand total Maou had outlined in the invoice was 500,000 yen. It was a figure that anyone could tell was all but insurmountable for an unemployed Emi.

The expenditures began with the salary loss Maou incurred for the regular work shifts he skipped. They continued with the fees for the two failed scooter exams, along with the cost for the upcoming third attempt. There was all the water, food, and camping gear they had bought for their journey into Ente Isla, along with the costs for a new phone to replace Maou's current one (which, shockingly, still worked). The biggest cost of all, however, was for the scooter itself.

Suzuno kept wincing as she ran down all the figures. Then she noticed something. "Devil King," she asked, "what does this line 'or three hundred fifty thousand yen—discuss' mean?"

"Ah, right. Well spotted, Suzuno. I wanted to negotiate with you a little too. The Gyros you bought—would it be okay if you gave me one?"

"What?"

"You said it was about five hundred thousand yen for two, right? I kinda like my bike, so I was thinking maybe I could forgive half of that in exchange for one."

The Honta Gyro-Roof vehicles Suzuno purchased boasted three wheels, industrial-level horsepower, a roof, and a lot of other features you didn't see in your typical scooter. Brand-new, it cost several times what a typical two-wheeler would run. Suzuno bought hers used, but they still ran to half a million yen total. Maou had driven one of them around Ente Isla, going so far as to call it "Mobile Dullahan III," but thanks to the assorted nonsense he got into over there, both of the Gyro-Roofs were still in Ente Isla. Emeralda and Albert said they would gather up all their neglected belongings and send them back to Japan, although that all still needed to be worked out.

"Half of that five-hundred-thousand-yen figure is the two hundred and fifty thousand for the Gyro, but if you aren't willing to let me have it, you know, I wouldn't mind some other model, either. I know these Gyros are hella expensive, but if I ain't picky, I can pick up a 50cc job for a hundred K or so. So I figure, hey, if you aren't giving me a Gyro, I figured we could set the total to three hundred and fifty thousand yen instead."

"...I refuse," Suzuno barked back, shaking her head. "I own both of those scooters, and once I have you repair the unauthorized beating you gave them, I intend to sell them back. With your demonic force, it should be a breeze to make them good as new, no?"

"Well, so be it!" Maou shouted, apparently expecting this. "Guess it'll be three hundred and fifty thousand then, Emi."

"Hold it, Devil King. This entire invoice is ridiculous in itself..."

Maou held a palm up to the cleric's face to stop her. "Butt out, Suzuno. If you won't let me have the Gyro, you've no part in this anyway. I didn't put in any of the money me and Acieth used that wasn't related to Emi. If you don't like it, well, I still got the receipts for the camping gear. I got documentation for every single thing on here, okay?"

"..." Emi fell silent, hand still clutching the handwritten receipt.

"Wait, you devil," Suzuno said, voice ratcheting up. "Whether you take my Gyro or buy your own, what basis do you have for making Emilia pay for your scooter? This is nothing like when I purchased a bicycle for you. If you had already owned a scooter and crashed it during the journey, that would be one matter, but this is just you having a childish desire for motorized transport!"

"Huh? What're you talking about?" Maou scoffed. "If that's how you're seeing it, I could always demand another reward, if you want."

"Reward?"

"Yeah. I mean, me, as long as Ashiya and Alas Ramus were okay, I would've gladly abandoned Emi over there. Maybe I played a big part with saving her dad's fields or whatever, but did you see anyone over there ordering me to get the Hero Emilia away from the Eastern Island?"

"No, but—"

"Emi and Alas Ramus are fused together, but if you think that means I wanted to save both of 'em equally, you're out of your mind, man. Alas Ramus is like a daughter to me, but Emi? She's my enemy, through and through."

"..." """

The two girls had no response for this fractured logic.

"So you see? I rescued my sworn enemy over there, and in exchange, all I'm asking for is a lousy, cheap little scooter. You should appreciate my generosity, instead of bitchin' at me all day."

This was jaw-dropping in two different ways. No matter how much griping he did on the way, to Suzuno, Maou seemed to show genuine concern for Emi during their journey. He was even kind enough to leave Emi to herself in Japan, until Nord woke up. He was right—this experience didn't mean Maou and Emi had kissed and made up. But did he really have to go on like this in front of Nord? It seemed terribly tacky of him.

"This is all too—"

"...All right. It's fine," Emi interrupted with a sigh as she nodded. "So this will settle it?"

"E-Emilia?!" a confused Suzuno fired back.

"If..." Emi looked straight at Maou. "If we're truly even with this, then it's a bargain, if anything."

Her voice was flat. Suzuno couldn't guess what drove her to say it. But as she looked at Maou, she realized that he was just as taken aback as she was. The response marked her total agreement to his terms—exactly what he wanted.

"Oh-*hohh*? Coming out swinging, huh? I'm talking three hundred and fifty thousand here, Emi, you heard it, right? Like, three hundred fifty thousand? And I only accept actual Japanese yen, minted by the Bank of Japan, all right?"

"Yes, I know," Emi said with a nod, retaining an air of calm. "What of it?"

"What of...? Like..." Maou, for his part, had lost all sense of calm. "Um, are you good for it, or...?"

"What do you want? You're the one demanding it, aren't you? I know I owe you one. I'll pay it."

"Oh...um, really?"

"But come back once you work this part out."

"Eh, which part?"

Emi tapped on the line that included the scooter. "This is just a guesstimate, right? Find out how much the scooter you want's gonna be, work out the insurance and all that stuff, then put all that on the invoice."

"Uh, yeah... Sure, um..."

Maou nodded several times as he took the invoice back.

"Is that all?"

"Uh, uhmm…yeah," he awkwardly replied.

"All right. So, not to be rude, but could you leave me alone? I'm gonna have to go shopping for a lot of things."

"S-sure thing. Sorry."

The monotone flatness of Emi's voice made the tension of the past ease as Maou cautiously left Room 101, the picture of dejection.

"Maou," Suzuno said to his back—"…!"—only to fall silent once more.

There was something in his back pocket—a thin magazine, rolled up and folded every which way after he sat on it—and it made her lose her voice.

"Ugh… This is what happens when you keep doing things in the most roundabout way possible."

Boarding the train that rolled into Eifukucho station, Suzuno sighed as she sunk into a seat, not bothering to care about the wrinkles it'd put on her kimono's belt.

A week had passed since that initial invoice. The scooter price was still TBD, Maou unable to come to a firm decision, but Emi had already bought him a new phone and paid him for the past two failed scooter license exams, the camping equipment, and half of the week's worth of part-time shifts he missed. That just left the other half of his salary, but as far as Nord could tell, Emi's bank account was firmly at zero.

He wondered how she drained it that fast, even with everything she owed to Maou, but apparently Emi said she had another debt to repay to Emeralda as well. These were the travel expenses she borrowed from her immediately after reaching Ente Isla. She had promised to repay it, and as she insisted to Nord, she simply had to follow through on that. Emeralda wasn't going to harangue her for it the way Maou did, of course; it didn't need to be paid back, and so there was no particular deadline. But every time the topic came up, Emi said the same thing: "If I don't settle everything, I can't move on."

Gently jostled by the train, Suzuno gave a tragic look to Nord, his head currently in his hands. He, too, knew that Maou was Satan, king of the demons, the man who made Ente Isla suffer for his self- ish goals. But given how involved the elder Justina was with the Yesod fragments long before Emi and Suzuno knew about them, he couldn't find it in himself to peg Satan as his sworn enemy. Instead, he agonized over the fact that this loan shark was bilking Emi for everything she had—and she accepted it, refusing any help to boot. It would put any parent in a bind.

"I suppose," Suzuno said to herself, "the future Chiho wants is still a faraway thing, no matter how close it may seem."

Indeed. A world conquest that involved the Hero and Devil King on friendly terms? Would there be no realizing that teenager's dream, the result of her honest love for both of them? As Suzuno pondered over it, the Keio Inokashira Line train stopped at Meidai- mae station. It was time to transfer to another line.

"For now, Nord, let's just focus on getting your belongings in order."

"Yes..."

If the far-flung future seemed too ominous to consider, it was always better to focus on the things in front of you. Such was the thought on Suzuno's mind as the two of them boarded a train bound for Keio Hachioji station.

✷

Later that afternoon...

Rika Suzuki was staring up at an apartment building, following the map on her smartphone. Her eyes opened wide. It was *luxe*, that much was·clear.

"Maaaan, she's got a nice place..."

She was headed for Room 505 of Urban Heights Eifukucho, an apartment that was several levels above Rika's one-room walk-up over in Takadanobaba.

"Is that, like, a penthouse on the top floor? Wow! What made her want to live in a place like this, I wonder?"

The exterior was shocking enough. The presence of a condo-style lobby turned her eyes into saucers.

"I bet she'll have one hell of a story for me today."

Putting her phone into her shoulder bag, Rika repositioned the souvenir box of cream puffs inside and walked through the front entrance, more than a little excited.

She was here to see Emi, to have her tell the story of her life, and of Ente Isla—a world Rika still couldn't will herself to fully believe. It had been just over a week since the missing Emi returned home, and now that things had settled a bit, Emi found it time to invite her good friend over.

As she went inside, Rika spotted someone by the entrance, in front of the intercom. A resident, perhaps? A small woman wearing a beret and a bag that looked too big for her slight figure. Rika paid her little mind, but the moment the automatic doors whizzed open to greet her, the girl whirled around.

"Um, I apologize for the awkward quessstion..."

"Y-yes?" Rika half-shouted, startled.

"I needed to see someone in this builllding, but the door on this side won't ooopen for me..."

"Oh."

The woman with the strange drawl didn't look too terribly concerned as she pointed out the automatic glass door leading into the apartment hallway.

"It says 'automaaatic' on it, but it won't even open maaanually for me. What should I dooo?"

Well, duh. It's an auto-lock door. You're supposed to call someone on the intercom to have them open it.

"Oh, um, you can use this panel to call a room..."

"Call...a roooom?"

The small woman arched her eyebrows, looking genuinely puzzled.

"Well, I mean, you use this keypad to type in a room number, and then you press the 'call' button to have them open up for you."

"Ooh, reeeally?" The woman gave a glance at Rika, then the panel, looking a little surprised. "I thought there was some secret cooode I had to get."

We got a weird one here, Rika thought.

"Y-yeah. Well, hopefully that helps. You can go ahead."

"Umm, s-sorrry again..."

"Yes?"

"It looks like the numbers only go from zero to niiine... What do you do if you want to put in a number higher than thaaat?"

"...Huh?" Rika murmured, unsure what she was being asked.

"Well, I want to visit Room 505, but there's no '505' button here, sooo..."

As if there would be. It was odd to the extreme, running into someone in the twenty-first century who didn't know how to operate a number pad. But the look of surprise Rika gave the woman was for another reason.

"Um, what is iiit?"

"Did you say Room 505?"

"Mm-hmm."

Rika took a moment to scan the clothing this woman wore, from top to bottom. The main thing it told her was that she was...well, different. In a way Rika couldn't quite put into words. It seemed to her like the fancy-looking outfit, as well as the bag under her shoulder, were made with some sort of traditional techniques, and not the kind you saw often in Japan. And she didn't know why she hadn't picked up on it before now, but the hair protruding from under the beret—and the eyes staring at Rika right now—were both a beautiful shade of bluish green, something no Japanese person would be naturally sporting.

The look made Rika recall someone in her memory.

"Um, you wouldn't be...Emeralda, would you?"

"Y-yesss?!" the petite woman squeaked, taking a surprised step back. "And, and youuu are...? Have we met somewhere beforrre? You're native to Japaaan, right?"

"N-no, um, we haven't met exactly, but..." Rika took a step back of her own, peering intently at the woman. "I heard from a girlfriend

of mine that Emi used to have a friend who was really short, with green hair, and spoke with kind of a drawl. She said her name was Emeralda…um, Emeralda…"

"Emeralda Etuuuva." The woman peered up at her. "Wow, what a surpriiise! And 'Emi' is Emilia's name in Japan, riiight? Does that mean you're Rika Suzuuuki?"

"Yep, sure am. Did Emi tell you about me?"

"Well, sooometimes Emilia talks about people on the phooone, so…"

"Huh. Kinda funny how we knew about each other through two different people." Rika smiled and typed "505" into the keypad.

"By the waaay, this 'girrrlfriend' of yours…" Emeralda gave Rika a look as she pressed the call button. "Could it be Chiho Saaasaki? Or Suzuno Kamazuuuki, maybe?"

"Yeah, pretty much." Rika gave a distracted smile. "Not that I should be crowing about this, but we've gone through a bunch of stuff, and I kinda got caught up in it a bit ago. Like, about Ente Isla, and things. I came here because Emi—er, Emilia—said she wanted to give me the whole story from the start, but I wasn't expecting another Ente Islan visitor, too! Or did Emi schedule this today 'cause you'd be around?"

"Nooo, I don't think so. In fact, I don't think she—"

"Hi, Rika!" came the sudden cheerful voice from the intercom. *"I'll buzz you in right…um. Is that Eme over there?!"*

"Hello! Sorry for the lack of noootice."

Emeralda smiled and waved at the camera next to the keypad that Rika helpfully pointed out to her.

"Wait, so… What're the two of you doing?"

She must have been right, Rika thought. Emi had no idea she was here. She and Emeralda gave each other wry smiles and looked at the camera. "We just ran into each other," they said simultaneously, Emeralda extending out the final "r" sound a bit.

"…"

This really *was* a fancy apartment. So fancy that the advanced intercom system even picked up on Emi's silent trembling.

* * *

"This is a total surprise. You never said you were coming, and all of a sudden you're all buddy-buddy with Rika..."

Still unable to hide her shock, Emi brought some freshly brewed tea.

"You sure you've never met each other?"

"Well, through other peeeople," Emeralda said with a smile, borrowing Rika's turn of phrase.

"Now I'm really starting to wonder what you've been saying about me," Rika added with a friendly elbow to Emi's side.

"Um, n-nothing bad or anything!" She looked to Emeralda for assistance.

"I think she said 'aaaffable'? Real 'clean-cut' and 'chill,' whatever that meeeans."

"Yeah, I'm sure you aren't too familiar with those terms. Quite an honor, though!"

"Hee-hee! Ohh, but I wonderrred... Did Sasaki and Bell say anything about meee?"

"I just heard a little bit before Maou and Suzuno went to Ente Isla. Just, like, general stuff about you. Chiho gave me a quick rundown of Emi's life in Maou—I mean, the Devil King Satan's apartment, and that's when I heard about you."

"Ooh, don't worry, I know all your Japanese naaames, too. So what did they saaay about me?"

"Well, you and...Albert, right? You were both old friends of Emi's, and you were this really cute and powerful sorceress or whatever. Like, as powerful as Emi. And that's about it, actually."

"Aww! Sasaki is so niiice." Emeralda gave a satisfied smile as she sipped.

"Oh, also she said you eat a lot for your size."

"...Mmm... Well, I have no excuse for thaaat, I guess."

The truth apparently hurt. Or, at least, hurt enough to make Emeralda freeze for a moment—something that didn't escape the other two girls' notice.

"But it's just because all the food here is so goood," Emeralda continued as her eyes swiveled over to the souvenir box on the table.

"Heh. Good thing I bought a party-size box," Rika said as she opened it up.

"...Um, what aaare those?" Emeralda said as she saw the light, flaky, cream-laden pastries lined up inside.

"Cream puffs. You don't know 'em?"

"Creeeam...?"

"Yeah, I guess I just fed you some regular cake last time you came," Emi said. "Do you need a fork or something?"

"You don't eat a cream puff with a fork, Emi! A real woman just chomps right into 'em."

"Is it kind of like breeead?"

"Not...bread, exactly, I don't think. But try it. It's from this joint that just opened in Takadanobaba. It's so full of college students all the time, it's hard to get in sometimes!"

"Mmm..."

Like a cat cautiously pawing at a new and unfamiliar toy, Emeralda half-stared at the cream puffs before slowly taking one in hand.

"Oooh, so liiight...but it feels heavy insiiide?"

"Don't hold it so tight like that. You'll squirt all the cream out."

Emeralda nodded, still intently gazing upon the confection.

"Here we gooo!"

With a final drawl, she took a big bite of the rather large cream puff with her small mouth. The next moment, her eyes opened up as much as humanly possible.

"It's soooooooooooooooooo *goooooooooooooooooooooooood*!!"

"Whoa!"

The squeal of ecstasy had a sort of bloodcurdling effect to it that honestly startled Rika.

"So liiight! And melllty! And sweet! And, ugghhh, so *liiight* again!"

"Again?"

Emi and Rika gave her confused looks before Rika slammed a fist on her own palm.

"Ohh, I bet that's the vanilla bean aroma doing its work on ya."

"Ahh, that makes sense."

"That's a regular custard cream puff you're eating right now, but the ones wrapped in that yellow paper have sweet-potato cream. That's an autumn exclusive."

The description made Emeralda's eyes sparkle anew.

"Emiliaaaa!!"

"...All right, all right. We can buy some later. As long as you don't mind somewhere local to me."

"Hooraaaaaaaaay!!!"

The sight of Emeralda reaching for a second puff while her mouth was still full of the first one made Rika smile and shrug. "I tell you," she said, "if I weren't actually seeing all you guys, I'd never believe this Hero and Devil King and grand sorceress crap for a second."

Emi and Emeralda exchanged glances.

"So, um, I know we all got a little distracted, but what brought you here all of a sudden, Eme?"

"Fwuhh?"

"It's got to be something really important if it's you personally coming over."

"Fwore hwfhh. Arr-hhoo hafwuff wffuu hurrh woofooo."

The alien language came from the supremely satisfied mouth of Emeralda after she took a big bite of the second cream puff.

"Ooh, but the pastries on this planet are so *goood*," she managed after a moment, wiping the powdered sugar off her lips and taking a big swig of tea. "Welll, the reason I'm here is because I have something to reporrrt to you, Emilia."

"Report?"

"Mm-hmm. I apologize for interrupting you and Rikaaa, but I think it probably connects with what you wanted to talk to herrr about."

She quietly placed her teacup on the saucer.

"Olbaaa," she continued in the same tone of voice, "well, he's been taaalking."

"What?!"

"Whoa!"

Emi shot to her feet, almost kicking the table over in the process. It was up to Rika to keep it upright.

"So I thought I'd repcrrrt to you on what we know right now." Emeralda turned to Rika. "Is that all riiight?"

"Well, if it's that important, you can go ahead first," she said with a nod. "I'm just butting in more than anything."

"Thank youuu! ...Ahem!" she coughed as she bowed. Then she narrowed her eyes and looked at the surface of her half-full cup of tea. Seeing the look in her eyes made Rika instinctively hold her breath a moment. This was no longer the sugar-craving little girl with cartoon hearts shooting out of her with every bite of Rika's cream puffs. It was the face of a master-level sorceress from a world Rika couldn't even fathom.

"The root of his betrayal," she began in an uncharacteristically tense voice, "is far greater, and far deeper, than any of us imagined."

—At first, Albert and I both assumed that Olba's betrayal began after he started sheltering Lucifer. The fact Lucifer even existed, after all, indicates that the "angels" in our holy scriptures were real all along. There are many Church records about clerics attempting to communicate with the angels, but none of them give positive proof that angels exist, or that anyone has ever traveled to the heavens.

We had thought the Great Demon General calling himself a "fallen angel" was simply a poetic turn of phrase. But he looks notably human, and he bore the same supernatural wings as the scriptures described. I would not describe myself as particularly devout, but the sight of him was enough to startle even me. To Olba, one of the six archbishops who led the entire Church, it must have come as an incomparable shock.

I'm not sure you are aware of this, Rika, but Sadao Maou's roommate, Hanzou Urushihara, is the original fallen angel described in our scripture, bearer of the original sin, the man who attempted to become as a god, the child of the dawn, and, well, a lot of other things. The most famous of all the angels.

I know, judging by what Emi told me about his antics on Earth, this might be difficult to believe. He doesn't help with chores, he doesn't work, he throws garbage all over the place, and he uses the Devil King's money to buy stuff.

Mm, yesss, well, aaanyway, you'll have to accept that Hanzou Urushihara is a pretty famous figure in Ente Isla's holy texts or else we aren't gonna get aaanywhere with this, so just ignorrre his current bad habits for me, all riiight? He went from angel to deeemon, so I doubt he's ever had to lift anything heavier than a spoon all his liiife. *Ooh*, this puff is good.

Um, so I was talking about how I think Lucifer's presence shocked Olba a lot. After Lucifer was defeated in Ente Isla, we continued our journey, Olba acting no different from before. We went with Albert to defeat Adramelech on the Northern Island and Malacoda on the Southern Island. Then we drove Alciel off the Eastern Island, and from there, that led to the final battle in Devil's Castle.

During that fight on the Central Continent, Olba pretended to chase after the fleeing Satan and Alciel, pushed Emilia into a closing Gate, and went his separate way from us. After the Gate swallowed Emilia up, Albert and I talked things over with him.

The decision we made still pains to me to this day. Albert insisted that we should pursue Emilia at once, but Olba and I thought it best to wipe up the remaining Devil King's Army forces and make sure we were prepared before we tracked her down. Emilia was powerful enough to completely overwhelm both the Devil King and Alciel at the same time. We didn't expect the Gate to lead to another world like this one, and after placing all our trust on that power, the sight of us pursuing her in a panic would crush the morale of all the knights who joined us in that Devil's Castle duel.

So Albert eventually agreed with Olba and me, and we switched tactics to joining the Federated Order of the Five Continents and sweeping up the powerful demons who remained in the land.

…Indeed, at the time, both of us trusted Olba with all our hearts.

At times of peace, Olba would have been a political enemy of mine, both as a high-level Church cleric and as a secular bureaucrat. But during our journey, whether fighting or not, Olba's strength, knowledge, and kindness saved us more times than I could ever count. That is why the shock we felt when we realized he tricked us is so impossible to put into words.

Once the main resistance was taken care of, Albert and I made our way from the Federated Order base to the nearest Stairs to Heaven, hoping to track the path that the Devil King and Alciel's Gate had traced. We did our best to find Emilia, but I am afraid that it took a great deal of time. We had no idea they had all been taken to another world, after all. That, and tracing her path was mainly Olba's work—for all we know, he could've been feeding us false information the whole time.

As you know, Emilia, Olba lured us to Sankt Ignoreido, claiming he had found you, only to hold us captive there. He then released Lucifer, whom he had secretly been nursing back to health, and traveled to Japan to assassinate you.

I think the Devil King has already told you why Olba brought Lucifer in for that mission. Olba, along with the Church, the Federated Order, and many other kingdoms, were afraid their people would turn toward Emilia as their next unifying force. They were already seeing it happen in the world, and there is no denying the fact that Crestia Bell was sent to Earth in part for that reason.

But regardless of Ente Isla politics, I think there is ample room for doubt in this story. It is worth remembering, as the Church continues to insist, that Emilia's rank was "Church knight" when she departed on her journey. As an archbishop, Olba could have put her under his guardianship, or canonized her, or done any number of things to ensure her powers were kept under the auspices of the Church. She may not act it all the time, but Emilia often finds it easy to go with the flow, instead of being assertive for herself. If she was convinced it would help the people, she might have taken up the offer willingly, for all I know.

But either way, I felt Olba lacked the motivation he would've needed to fear the rise of Emilia's political currency that much. In fact, Olba didn't try to lure Emilia in with money or the like—he used her father's fields as a hostage. So when I asked him about my doubts, he began to say all sorts of interesting things.

You would be surprised. In our custody, he aged astoundingly quickly, in the course of a single week. His hair turned bright white in the blink of an eye; he once wore a tonsure, as you know. His holy magic has been fully sealed off, and he is under round-the-clock surveillance by a team of forty-five elite soldiers, including some magicians. It goes without saying that we aren't giving him access to razors or other sharp implements, and as a result, his hair is starting to get rather long. He always *did* take such fine care of himself. Still a bishop, I suppose, at the core.

Mmmm!

Now, of courrrse, I'm not willing to accept everything he told me as the unvarnished truuuth. Little of it is verifiable, or at least easily so. So that's why I dropped by like this. To, you know, receive a little adviiice from you and the Devil King, since you have so much more experience with angels and the heaaavens...

"Your drawl's coming back, Eme."

"Oooh, ummm, I was trying not to sound caaasual since this was a serious conversation, but it's hard to keep up for looong...so..."

"That's one heck of a transformation," Rika remarked as Emeralda took a breath and sat back, relaxing against the table.

"So you're saying this betrayal runs deep, based on what Olba told you?"

"Ah, yesss," Emeralda continued, face still turned downward. "I guess since looong before the Devil King's Arrrmy invaded, Olba was conviiinced that heaven and the angels existed. Not because he was a Church clerrric, but I guess because he actually saaaw it for himself."

"For himself?"

"I meeean, he saw that heaven isn't where souuuls go, or where you end up when you diiie, or some metaphyyysical thing like thaaat, but a place that really exiiists, that you can physically gooo to, and, and stuuuff..."

"...Eme?"

"Uh-huhhh?"

"You can have my cream puffs, too, all right? So just keep—"

"But being a cleric also meant he was—*munch, chew*—blocked by the restraints of our scripture and his Church duties, so he didn't have any real method—*gulp, slurp*—of researching heaven or proving it really existed—*gobble*."

It was a breathtaking revival. Picking up Emi's cream puffs one by one and aligning them in both her grubby mitts, she ate them all, switching from hand to hand. Then her eyes slowly stiffened once more, as she returned to "serious" mode.

"Emeralda, there's cream and sugar all over your cheeks."

Rika, floored by Emeralda's force of will a moment ago, was now using a wet tissue to wipe the grand sorceress's face. The dignity and majesty of the high-level magician was now just as much a thing of the past as the sugary desserts churning in her stomach.

—So I told you about how Olba was convinced that heaven existed. The reason he was so sure? The Holy Silver housed at the core of the sword Emilia wielded. Thank you, Rika. Let me have some tea first... Whew.

Now, as you know, Olba's Church duties included supervising our diplomatic and missionary efforts. He had gone on many missionary trips himself, from a young age, and thus he knew the god he believed in wasn't necessarily the one true, matchless one out there. If he was, then why were so many in the world oblivious to his existence? How could these people live, and build entire nations, without knowing this god was watching over them? Our scripture talks about the glories of spreading the word of our god to those who believe in other religions, but in that case, why did the Church have to wield so many bloody battles against sovereign nations for the sake of this? These so-called missionary wars?

During his travels, Olba encountered a great deal of fully matured nations. He knew there were many not so willing to accept the god he taught at face value. The concept of forcing them to recognize this god by swordpoint was, as he said, a constant source of concern for him.

Then he stumbled upon a major contradiction. The old adage of "loving thy neighbor," a phrase even a child knows, directly contradicts much of the Church's actual history. What kind of god would brand those who refuse their teachings as evil, giving them permission to kill those who refuse to bend to its will? He realized that many bishops of the past arbitrarily interpreted the absoluteness of our god as approval of massacring the neighbors we should have loved, in the name of that god himself. Those bishops saw this as a divine purge; they said the souls of the slain would be purified by those who believed, that our god would save them from pain and hatred.

But what Olba saw was different. He saw people who never forgot about the massacres and plunder the Church selfishly carried out · for centuries. Instead, they kept the story alive across generations. He encountered those who said the god Olba worshipped was evil incarnate. Even in this modern world, where we try to debate our differences instead of fight to the death over them, Olba found his divine teachings fall upon deaf ears.

It made him realize another contradiction in his life. You could say that he began to doubt his god existed at all.

Looking back at the scripture, Olba realized his god had made all kinds of mistakes. The only thing that went fully according to plan was the creation of the world, and the life that thrived on it. After that, he let evil make its way into paradise, watched mankind succumb to temptation and betray him over and over again, and sat on the side as the very creatures he created warred endlessly with one another. They even dared to create gods besides himself! All of this, as the Church swore that their god was the only "true" one.

This absolute font of everything good, making mistake after mistake, and we still worship him anyway. How could such a bundle of contradictions be a god at all? Only a human could be capable of such a thing, Olba thought.

And, as he put it to me, it was this realization that drove him to advance through the ranks of the Church. If every move the Church made was by the hand of fallible men and women, all he had to do was remember that, and act based upon it. He hadn't fully abandoned his conscience as a Church cleric at this point, but I would be hesitant to call him particularly "devout" after that, either.

I think the best way to describe Olba is as a master strategist. He is completely versed in the politics, the economics, and the laws of the Church, a vast nation whose fortunes lie not in the land it possesses but in the hearts and minds of those it takes hold of. He is a genius at reading, and controlling, human nature.

And when he finally was promoted to archbishop, that granted him access to something he never had before: Holy Silver. The holy vestments of Sankt Ignoreido, supposedly granted to them by an angel from heaven. He knew the tale of the Hero appearing when evil threatens the world, bearing a sword made from this blessed metal, and now he saw it for himself. It made Olba realize that both "heaven" and "angels" were real, palpable things. All of it—the Church, its scripture, the holy metal itself—existed on the same plane as mankind.

This apparently made Olba have a thought:

"Perhaps *I* can become a god, then."

Emi shrank back, face pallid, as if she was hearing Olba's raspy voice in her own apartment.

"He really thought that...?"

"It seems so, yes. The thing the kingdoms and other bishops feared the most was, quite literally, you—or, to be exact, the thought of you horning in on their own interests. Olba, on the other hand, had another, deeper concern."

"…That I'd become a god? With my Holy Silver, and my Yesod fragment?"

"I believe so."

"How could he be so…ridiculous…?" Emi crossed her arms, shaking a little, as Rika gave her a reassuring pat on the back.

"After he touched the Holy Silver for the first time, Olba scoured the world for signs of other supernatural phenomena, believing the Silver not to be a solitary relic. It had been examined and investigated by the seminary and other bishops for years, and the Church had long concluded that it was not of this world. But now, Olba believed, the whole concept of 'not of this world' was invalid—the Holy Silver was right here, at his fingertips. He had full access to this metal, along with the time and money required to give it a thorough investigation. So he did—constantly, ever since he became a bishop. But he never found anything else of a similarly divine nature on Ente Isla. It must have unnerved him, having no leads and fighting against time and old age. And then…that very thing happened."

Emi looked up. "The Devil King's Army…?"

"Yes—and with that, talk of the prophesied Hero bearing the Holy Silver. It filled Olba with joy, since as he saw it, a Hero who could wield this material would be invaluable for his own research. He didn't see the Hero as a mere prophecy but as a real, palpable thing, planned out by somebody long ago. He truly believed that, and then it happened. Emilia Justina, the fabled Hero of divine blood."

"…"

"You okay, Emi?"

"Y-yeah… I'm sorry, Rika. Stay with me a moment."

"I'm right here," she said, sidling up a little.

"It was apparently rather simple," Emeralda continued, "to find you. That's because the Church had a certain ritual it carried out upon the Holy Silver whenever darkness threatened the world. A simple one—the correct person, in this case a high-level Church cleric, infusing the right amount of holy energy into the Silver. As the story went, the metal would then provide a guiding light to the Hero's location."

It sounded familiar to Emi. She had seen just such a light many times before, a light she even thought she was emitting herself. It wasn't until later that she would realize the light was simply Yesod fragments pulling against each other—a fact that the Church remade into a nice, holy-sounding tale for its own benefit. But who spread that tale? Where did it come from? There was only one possibility.

"Laila..."

Her mother had set up the whole thing. This massive, cross-planetary farce over the Yesod fragments.

"So the Church found you, Emilia, and took you to their head-quarters in Sankt Ignoreido. But at the time, Olba's ambitions were still small-scale, focused upon observing you around the Holy Silver and applying the results to his research. What decisively changed his mind was the moment you touched the Silver for the first time."

"The first... What do you mean?"

"Do you remember? The Hero in the prophecy is the 'Hero of the *Holy Sword.*'"

"...Oh."

"But the girl they brought before the Holy Silver manifested a lot more than a sword."

Emi gasped. She realized that the point Emeralda was guiding her toward involved the deepest core tenets of her life.

"The Cloth...of the Dispeller...!!"

"Whoa, Emi, you still with me?" Rika exclaimed as Emi hugged her even tighter, trying to calm her down. "You wanna take a break? 'Cause I'm still new to all this, and this is pretty heavy for me, too. Taking it all at once would stress anybody out, so..."

"...I'm fine. I'm fine, so... Please. I need to hear all of it."

"...All right," Emeralda said, balancing her concern over Emi's mental state and her belief that she could handle it. "Seeing the sword and Cloth delighted Olba—and unlike the other bishops, he didn't assume the Cloth was simply part of the package, so to speak, with the sword. He was shocked to see it, but he brought an analytical approach to the question. The things he wanted more than anything else in the world were now right in front of him. To Olba, the sword and the Cloth of the Dispeller were both precious samples of Holy Silver. He apparently thought the guiding light everyone saw was the Holy Silver and the Cloth attracting each other.

"Thus Olba volunteered to serve as Emi's guardian, taking advantage of his extensive missionary experience to assume a leadership role when it came time to fight the Devil King.

"Seeing the two holy vestments you manifested confirmed to Olba that he was right—that heaven and angels really exist. And on the day Saint Aile was liberated, Olba finally encountered him for the first time—incontrovertible proof that angels were living, breathing things. In other words, the Great Demon General Lucifer."

"And that was...what led him to..."

"Lucifer was almost dead after fighting you, and Olba saved him—only pretending to strike the lethal blow. It was his first real step toward trying to become a physical god. The theories he formulated over the years were proven all too true by the Devil King's Army invasion. But there was one disappointment for him—Lucifer knew nothing about Holy Silver, or Emilia's weapon."

That had bothered Emi before. Essentially, Lucifer—Urushihara—acted like he was completely oblivious about her sword. He was an archangel on the class of Sariel and Gabriel—maybe higher than that, given how early he showed up—and all the Yesod-fragment stuff was news to him. Why was that?

"Still, as far as Olba was concerned, Lucifer was a vital tool in bringing him down the road to divinity. So he kept him safe, even as he traveled with you—and just as all of you stormed Devil's Castle, Olba saw the guiding light again."

"Yes... My sword, reacting to the Alas Ramus core that the Devil King was holding."

"This, apparently, was a cause of concern for Olba. There was a new sample nearby, that much he knew, but if you defeated the Devil King and seized it for yourself, that would no doubt grant you yet more power. The kind of power that could make a god, or an angel, want to call you home."

A Hero's position was assured as long as she was actively fighting for the human world. But when the evil is smited and the Hero's strength is no longer required, all that power could easily provide the spark for new, untold chaos. Would that be all right with whoever granted the sword and Cloth of the Dispeller to the world? Would he or she want to have more people coming close to the secrets they held?

To Olba, who wanted to avoid any possibility of this precious path to the heavens closing on him, the Devil King and Alciel fleeing the planet was a stroke of fantastic good luck. Alas Ramus's core was left behind in Devil's Castle, but if Olba could get both Emilia and this Devil King who somehow reacted to her out of this world, that would earn him more precious research time. So he pretended to pursue the Devil King, only to shut off the Gate early once Emilia was through it—and he successfully hid his intentions from Emeralda, Albert, and the entire Federated Order on the scene. What he wasn't expecting was that they'd all be taken to another planet. Tracking them down took a vast amount of time.

"After that, Emilia, you know the rest of the story. Olba and Lucifer sowed the seeds of chaos in Japan, attempting to defeat the Hero and Devil King for their own nefarious aims. But out of all the errors of judgment Olba made, the biggest one of all was failing to imagine that you and the Devil King would not only make contact, but even get along with each other."

"...Kind of rough to have it put *that* way." Emi smiled, the blood still drained from her face.

"Thus, at the very last moment, Olba failed to kill you. It cost him Lucifer and the ability to return to Ente Isla, and it closed off his path to divinity...or it should have, anyway."

"...Was it Sariel? Gabriel? Or Raguel?"

Emeralda grinned at the barrage of questions. "It was Sariel, at first, he said. Sariel helped him escape custody in Japan, and after that, he aided the heavens in the search for Yesod fragments, under their close supervision. He also told me that speaking with angels besides Lucifer made him change his ways of thinking, a little."

Sariel and the other angels wielded untold amounts of force, far greater than anything Satan, the Devil King, or Emilia the Hero had. They had physical strength, a divine mystique, holy-power reserves that no mere human could ever approach, and overwhelming intelligence. The sight of them filled Olba with awe—and then, convinced he had won their favor, he began to serve as their willing puppet. He hadn't given up on his divine aspirations, but after their battle in Sasazuka, Olba's goalposts had shifted a bit. Now, even if he wasn't an absolute god, he still hoped to become an angel with strength like Sariel's or Gabriel's—strength that would let him become a physical symbol of worship on Ente Isla.

But now—his overambitious plans unraveled, his divine hopes crushed by the force of Maou, Emi, and Suzuno—Olba was a shell of a man, drained of both the light of ambition and the force of life itself.

"Listening to all that," Rika interjected, "I mean, I'd say he had it coming. There was no saving him for what he did. But what's gonna happen to that guy now? Do they have the death penalty over there or anything?"

Emeralda dejectedly shook her head. "I cannot say yet. We would need to figure out which country's laws have jurisdiction over him, or if any law, indeed, could fully address his actions. Even after all this, he remains an archbishop and 'close friend' of the Hero. Condemning him to death would have far too great an impact."

The wrinkles between her eyebrows deepened, betraying how much the thought anguished her.

"I doubt we will come to any conclusion in very short order. We were rather surprised, honestly, to see Olba confess so much to us so quickly. I imagine the Devil King appearing in Efzahan, confounding his plans, and defeating the angels came as quite a shock to him. But we still don't know why he was working with the angels to have Emilia and Alciel fight each other over there, and... Still all right, Emilia?"

Emeralda sighed as she peered at her friend.

"I'm not so sure, anymore," Emi replied, "but at least I know a few more things now. And, you know, Chiho said something to me earlier…"

"Chiho Sasaki?"

"Yeah. My father said the same thing, too," she said, instinctively grasping Rika's hand. "From the start…probably since the moment I was born, I had the Better Half within me. I think the Holy Silver the Church retained bore the Cloth of the Dispeller, not the holy sword. Laila said she had given my father and me the 'key' to her own objectives. He and Acieth Alla were together the whole time—him, and the personification of the other holy sword… Sorry if I scare you, Rika."

Emi exchanged looks with her friend. Then she removed her hand and stood up, taking a step backward.

"And come to think of it, this Cloth has changed, too. Ever since I became one with this child."

She focused for a moment. "Whoa!" Rika exclaimed at what happened next. Amid a dazzling, bright light, a young girl appeared in Emi's arms—a girl with oddly colored hair, sleeping peacefully.

"Is that…Alas Ramus?"

She had never seen her quite this close, and she had certainly never seen a baby appear out of thin air before. But that wasn't all.

"And, uh… Emi? What's that outfit?!"

The other sudden change threw Rika for a complete loop, making her literally fall backward onto the floor.

The hair was a silken bluish gray, the crimson eyes piercing their way through any evil they spied. Over her casual dress was a full suit of armor, emitting a strange sort of sheen that lay somewhere between silver and a colorful prism.

"That's it…?" she murmured, surveying her friend. "The Hero?"

"Emilia, that shield…"

Emeralda was familiar with the transformation, but the Cloth of the Dispeller's new equipment came as a surprise.

"I didn't have this before," Emilia said, sizing up the round shield on her left arm a bit as Alas Ramus slowly stirred. "This is the Cloth, evolved. It happened after I fused with this child." She averted her eyes a bit. "My holy sword changes its form depending on how much holy energy I have. The Cloth transforms when it makes contact with a Yesod fragment, and making contact with Alas Ramus made it manifest a new shield. And her, and Acieth Alla… It makes *them* mature, as well."

She relaxed for a moment. Before Rika's eyes, the Cloth of the Dispeller was itself dispelled, forming bubbles of light that streamed back into Emi's body. Her hair and eyes were back to normal, and she was once more Emi Yusa, holding her child and taking her seat again, before a dumbfounded Rika.

"So the Yesod fragments each work their own way, but they have the ability to mature. Evolve. If that's what Laila is going for…then what happens once all the fragments are in one place?"

Emeralda and Rika had no answer for her.

"I don't know what Laila wants," she admitted. "I don't know what Gabriel and the heavens want, gathering all these children. But…no matter how it turns out, I don't want it to end unhappily for them." She turned to Emeralda. "I'm glad you came here today, Eme. Now I've got all the motivation I need for my next goal."

"What is that?"

"I'm still going to search for Laila, but not so I can find out what she wants. It's so I can be sure Alas Ramus has a happy future. My holy sword, my Cloth of the Dispeller—they're both precious partners of mine. I won't let Laila have her way with them."

"Whew!" Rika said, finally composed enough to pick herself up off the floor. "Seeing all this stuff in real life… Crazy!"

"You aren't…turned off by it?" Emi asked, giving her a concerned look.

Rika briskly shook her head, although the shock was still written clear upon her face. "Well, no, I just mean, wow, what a surprise! Like, man, what a friend I've got!" Then she sidled up to Emi on the couch, watching Alas Ramus as she began to squirm in her rapidly fading sleep. "Boy, seeing her up close, though… I can't really think of any other way to say this, but, like, seriously, she's cute as an angel.

I thought Acieth was pretty attractive herself, but a cute li'l kid like this is something else entirely!"

Her gaze focused on the resting child, then raised itself a little to settle upon Emi's face, where it lingered for a while. Emeralda observed this, declining to comment.

"And y'know, you two kinda resemble each other, actually. Like, in the eyes, and the shape of the mouth."

"Y-you think so? We really shouldn't, but…" Emi bashfully looked at the child. "You saying that makes me a little happy right now, I think."

"Yeah, but kind of… Maybe the forehead and eyebrows look a bit like Maou, though… Oh, um, too soon, maybe?"

Rika didn't mean it as a joke. But the response from the flushed Emi was sheer intimidation, as if she was silently spewing venom at her.

"Not 'too soon,' but… I appreciate what he did for me, but I haven't forgiven him at the root or anything, so… I don't know. It's complicated."

As far as Alas Ramus was concerned, Maou was her one and only father. Emi wasn't childish enough to pretend that wasn't the case. But that didn't change the fact that, even with his integral role in finding Nord, Maou had done more to smash up and ruin Emi's life than anyone else. And even though it seemed Laila was starting to have a bigger role in that than previously anticipated, as long as Maou declared himself king of all demons, she still believed that the atrocities of Maou's past were his, and his alone, to shoulder.

But she had already realized, by this point, that she could no longer kill Maou by herself. In fact, judging by the dreams she had of sharing a warm meal around his apartment's table again, Emi's subconscious had accepted a fairly large role for Maou in her life. It made her wonder whether it was worth finding reasons to keep hating him, or if taking the role of judge, jury, and executioner against him was even necessary.

"It's complicated," she repeated, as if reminding herself of the fact. "Good morning, Alas Ramus. Are you awake?"

"Mnngh… 'orrrrning…" The child rubbed her eyes, let out a cheek-stretching yawn, and turned her eyes around the room.

"!" When they settled upon Rika, her face snapped upward. In another moment, she was nimbly out of Emi's arms and hiding behind her back.

"Agh! Wh-what's up?"

"Oh, um, did I scare her?"

"Ah, right, she's never seen you before, has she?"

"Oooo," Alas Ramus murmured as she stole a furtive peek at Rika from behind, looking at her like she was a storybook wicked step-mother. Rika, not exactly used to small children, gave an awkward smile, wave, and "Hi?" It spooked Alas Ramus even more, into hiding her face fully behind Emi.

"Come on, Alas Ramus, you have to say hello. Where's your hello?"

"…Oo." She stuck her face out again, but timidly, the shock of an unfamiliar face right after she woke up still too much to deal with.

"Hmm, was Alas Ramus always as shyyy as this with new peeeople?"

"Hnn!!"

The voice from behind made the child literally fly into the air.

"A-Alas Ramus?!"

"Oh, uh, ah…?"

Like a jackrabbit, Alas Ramus leaped away from Emi's back. Now she was hiding behind Rika instead.

"Umm…"

The sensation of something small tugging at her shirt from behind made Rika feel incredibly ill at ease. She turned around.

"…Sis…?"

"Hmm? Hmmmm?"

Rika turned downward, sensing that Alas Ramus was saying something. Then she looked up and grinned awkwardly at Emeralda.

"She said, 'What's Eme-sis doing here?'"

"Ooooh…"

Emi looked at Emeralda, too, as she began to pout a little.

"She never was that big a fan of yours, huh, Eme?"

"Oh, come onnn! To the point where she's hiiiding behind some-one she's never met beforrre?"

"Can you blame her? You scared her with all that screaming and carrying on last time."

"And can you blame meee?" a dissatisfied Emeralda shot back. "A child this cute, I can't helllp but get a little louuuder."

Rika, meanwhile, waited for the small hands around her to ease up a little before daring to turn around.

"Um, hello?"

".........'lo," Alas Ramus whispered, realizing for the first time that she was latched on to a stranger. Mommy offered no further guidance.

"It's good to meet you, Alas Ramus."

"......yeh."

"Uh, my name's Rika Suzuki. I'm a friend of Emi... I mean, your mom."

"Suu-ki...?"

"Now, Alas Ramus, be polite to your big sis Rika, all right?"

"O, okeh, uh, hi, Riuh-sis."

The voice wasn't exactly enthusiastic, perhaps out of nervousness, but she still bowed with all her might at Rika.

"And hello to you, too! Man, Emi, what is this incredibly cute creature you've got here?" Rika could no longer prevent herself from breaking into a wide grin. "No wonder everyone's lining up to take care of you. And look at those tiny little hands!"

"Aph," the child replied as Rika grabbed one of them, looking toward Emi for help but still accepting the attention.

"And you know, Emi," Rika continued as she softly clasped both of Alas Ramus's hands, "I know you've had it rough for a while, and it's not gonna get easier very soon. So if you want someone to talk to, call me anytime, all right? Whether anything's happening or not. I'll keep looking for new lunch spots to take us to."

"...Rika."

"Rika...?"

"And when we meet up, be sure to bring Alas Ramus along, okay? Hey, Alas Ramus, what kind of food do you like to eat?"

"Corn soup 'n' curry!"

"Ooh, the classic kiddie one-two punch. Nice."

"And, an' Chi-sis's fried chicken!"

"Chi? Oh, you mean Chiho? She knows how to cook for kids like you, huh? I'm impressed! So you like fried chicken, curry, and corn soup, huh? I can think of a couple places along those lines, but if you want one that can pull off all three of those, I'll have to do some investigating. Can you even eat that much, though? You're still pretty small."

Rika didn't say anything else to Emi. She didn't need to. Emi already had everything she needed. Whether she was Emi Yusa or Emilia Justina, Rika just wanted to go out to eat with her. She wanted to talk about stuff. What more could she want?

"You have very good friends indeed, Emilia," Emeralda softly noted, making Emi's eyes moisten a little.

"Oh! And going out is fun and all, but what about a job, Emi? What're you gonna do about that? 'Cause you're gonna stay in Japan for a while, right? I mean, I doubt you're gonna be scraping at your bank account too quickly with the way you live, but it can't be cheap to live in an apartment like this, huh?"

Rika was always like that, diverting the conversation back to reality at just the right moment. Emi loved that.

"Oh, you'd be surprised. The rent here's fifty thousand yen."

"Huh?" Rika replied, wrinkling her face at the figure. "That's kind of crazy, isn't it? 'Cause between the size of this place and how close it is to the station, I would've figured at least twice that, easy."

Suzuno seemed equally surprised by the rent, when Emi revealed the figure to her. But to Rika, a veteran of urban living, the price took on a deeper, more concrete meaning. It was completely illogical to her.

"Yeah, well...if you want the truth, this apartment kinda had some...bad stuff go down inside it before I moved in, know what I mean?"

"Ewww! Really?"

Emi waved her hands in self-defense. "Oh! But, I mean, Rika, if it weren't for this joint, I probably wouldn't have gotten that job at Dokodemo, and I don't even know if I could've stayed afloat in Japan."

"Oh?"

"I've got a lot of memories associated with this place. I'll be living with my father again sometime, but moving out of here won't come cheap, so I think it'll be a while before I do that."

Rika turned to Emeralda, wondering if she knew more about this. The sorceress countered with a slight shrug.

"So, anyway, the rent's not really the problem. My finances are kinda rough right now, but I think I've got a line on a new job. I called this place that sounds like they need some fresh bodies ASAP, so we already have an interview set up. All I need to do is update the photo on my résumé."

"Ooh! The Hero at work, huh? Talk about takin' care of business." Rika smiled at this sunnier news. Then she gave her an incredulous look. Being her ex-coworker meant she had at least a vague idea of the salary Emi was pulling down. "But that rough already, huh? Something happen?"

"Well, kind of..."

Emi gave a quick summary of Maou and his invoice. It made both Rika and Emeralda wince.

"Oh, maaaaan..."

"Wowww."

"Devil King or not, is now really the time for that kinda thing?"

"Indeeed, this is kind of a disappoiiintment. I didn't think the Devil King *I* saw would act that waaay..."

Despite the criticism, the wry grin on Emi's face bore no evidence of anger or despair. "You think so, too?" she said. "Well, so did I. It's totally not like him."

"Oh?" both Emeralda and Rika said.

"I'm guessing he didn't think I'd accept his crazy terms at all, you know?" Emi stood up and took a magazine out from the shelf next to her TV. "But even I have a little bit of pride left. If I owe someone, I feel like I've got an obligation to pay them back myself. Plus..." She turned to a page that had a sticky note applied to it and showed it to them both. "If I completely fall for his conniving, I'll wind up owing him again."

Rika, reading the advertisement on the bookmarked page, stared in disbelief. "Ah, Emi, this is…"

Emi, expecting this, firmly nodded at the unspoken question, brimming with confidence.

"I've decided to apply here on my terms."

THE DEVIL AND
THE HERO GET
ALL HUNG UP ON
THEIR RELATIVE
POSITIONS

Early the next morning, Ashiya was roused out of his apartment and into the outside hallway by the sound of an engine. There was a midsize truck parked out front. Its container, bearing the logo of a moving company that advertised on TV all the time, was open, a pair of movers already removing boxes from it.

Suzuno and Nord were there, in the front yard, discussing matters with the moving staff, but Ashiya's focus lay elsewhere—upon the person standing next to them. He was watching Miki Shiba, owner of Villa Rosa Sasazuka and a woman whose body was akin to a giant, walking, metal-plated saké barrel.

"All right, Nord, this is the new key to Room 101. If you have any issues, feel free to contact Mr. Maou or Mr. Ashiya upstairs, or myself next door if they are indisposed."

"I do *not* remember taking on administrative duties, madam!!" Ashiya somehow found the courage to shout from above.

The three of them looked back up. Feeling Shiba's eyes upon him sent a chill up his spine, making him weak at the knees, like it always did. But they needed to settle things today, no matter what.

"Ah, hello there, Mr. Ashiya! Nord will be officially moving into Room 101 today, so I was just offering him the lay of the land."

"That's fine, madam, but I am neither the manager nor maintenance man for this building! If some kind of trouble occurs, I do not want it waiting on my doorstep!"

Ashiya could already feel his confidence wavering. But he felt his point was valid. Shiba had given that same line to Suzuno when she moved in, too. And while Shiba had been quite helpful with her arrangements back when Maou and Ashiya were new to Earth, Ashiya felt no obligation to assume further duties in return.

"Oh, no need to be such a fuddy-duddy," Shiba chirped. "In fact, I believe the management company told me that whenever something happened here, Mr. Maou always took the initiative to take feedback from the tenants and go through all the proper procedures?"

"Feedback?" Ashiya countered as he walked downstairs. "Ma'am, it was just us and Crestia Bell!"

"Well, perfect, then, isn't it? Always good to know your neighbors so intimately. And all of you share common roots in your homeland of Ente Isla, no less, am I right?"

"I would not describe our roots as 'common,' no! We are demons! Our upbringing and our lives are completely different!"

"Mm-hmm. And now you find yourselves all living under a common roof. Don't you think you're being rather unkind?"

Parrying Ashiya's complaints like an expert fencer, Shiba capped off her impromptu lecture with a wink. That was all it took for Ashiya's pulse to quicken. He felt faint.

"Gnnhh!"

"Um, is he all right?" a surprised Nord asked.

"They're always like this in front of the landlord," Suzuno explained as Ashiya clutched at his chest, breaking into a cold sweat. After taking a few deep breaths, he brought a hand to his brow and shook his head.

"My. Such inner strength!"

"Wh-what are you…talking about…? Well, enough about that for now. But, madam, would you please tell me already?"

"Tell you what?" Shiba replied, smiling as elegantly as ever. Ashiya lunged at the chance.

"Tell me where Urushihara's been admitted to!"

Not even this half-shouted order could dispel Shiba's gentle ease. "I told you," she said, "he is at the hospital owned by a friend of mine. If you are concerned about the cost, you really shouldn't be. Amane and I were the cause of this—"

"That is not what I am worried about!" Ashiya interrupted. "His computer is gone from our apartment!"

"His computer?" Shiba asked. "I apologize, were you the victim of a burglary recently?"

"?"

"Ahh," Suzuno said, picking up on the gambit even as it confused Nord.

"I only wish it were a burglar!!" Ashiya clenched his fists tightly. "Urushihara didn't take the computer with him to this hospital, did he?!"

Hearing the half-shouted question, Shiba elegantly brought a hand to her not-so elegant chin (or some layer of fat around it), as if recalling something. "Ah, yes," she began, "he was muttering something in his delirium about 'just the computer, just the computer,' so I do believe Amane took it with her, yes."

"H-how can this be?!!"

Ashiya looked and sounded like this meant the apocalypse was nigh. His knees shook, almost ready to collapse.

"Wait a moment, Alciel," Suzuno said, finally taking pity on him. "Most hospitals in Japan forbid you from using cell phones and electronic equipment, right? I highly doubt Lucifer is buying things off the Net with your card right now."

"N-no...? No. Indeed, you are correct, Bell. Perhaps I was overthinking this—"

"Mr. Urushihara was admitted into a special ward, so he can use all the computers and cell phones he wants. He can even keep watching TV after lights-out time."

"Whaaaaaaaaaaaaaaaatttt?!!"

"Whoa!"

The final condemnation from Shiba's lips made Suzuno's attempts at assuaging the demon useless. The ensuing wail of despair made Nord take a step back.

"Our card! I must cancel His Demonic Highness's credit card immediately! Bell! Lend me your phone! Our future is riding upon this! After all the danger we have overcome, the Devil King's Army is in mortal peril of collapse before it has even been restored!"

"Calm down, Alciel! Whether you live with him or not, you can't cancel the Devil King's credit card if he's not around!"

"Oh, the inhumanity! My liege has only just begun his shift, too... Noooooooooooooooooo..."

"Well, regardless, Nord, I am sure they will be enormously helpful neighbors to you!"

"Y-yes," Nord said, not exactly taking Shiba's reassurances at face value.

"W-wait... If I can get the paperwork together and bring it to his workplace... There's not a second to spare... I have to keep Urushihara's meddling hands away from my liege's bank account..."

Ashiya staggered his way back upstairs, like a translucent ghost, and returned to Room 201. He was out again quickly, almost breaking through the door as he tore downstairs and flew down the street. "My liiiiiiiiiiiege!!" he shouted as he went off, awing both Nord and the moving crew.

"Mr. Ashiya has certainly been through a lot, hasn't he?" the utterly disinterested Shiba observed. To Suzuno, who had an insider's view of life inside this ersatz Devil's Castle, she almost couldn't blame Ashiya for that reaction.

"So... Ms. Shiba?" she asked the hulking landlord once the screams faded from earshot.

"Yes?"

"The location where we'll be discussing matters..."

"Mmm?"

"Is there a reason why it's the hospital Lucifer was admitted to?"

The sharply pointed question did nothing to faze Shiba, as much as Suzuno wanted it to.

Ever since they all returned from Ente Isla, Shiba had offered them chances to discuss assorted matters with both herself and Amane. She set up specific times and places for these talks, but there were more than a few strange things about them. One, she wanted to hold the next one at Urushihara's hospital—whose location she was still keeping a secret. Two, whenever these discussions came up in conversation, Chiho seemed to clam up, a dark cloud descending upon her countenance. Suzuno thought she had just imagined it at first, but upon closer observation, she realized she was right—Chiho was concerned over something, although she never said what. It seemed likely Shiba and Amane told her about a few choice matters while everyone else was on Ente Isla.

"Oh," Shiba replied, "no great reason, no. I just thought it would reduce the burden on Mr. Urushihara, is all."

"If anything, some more burden to his life would do wonders, I think..."

Suzuno shrugged. It would take more than this attack for Shiba to leak out anything else to her.

"Hey!" a voice rang out from across the front road. "Pop! Suzuno! Hmm? That was Ashiya? Why he so in the hurry?"

"Mm..."

"Ah, Acieth."

They turned to find Acieth heading their way—Alas Ramus's "little" sister, a fellow Yesod-fragment personification, and the core of a second Better Half.

"I thought maybe the boxes are here, so I come to see."

"Thanks." Nord nodded, bowing his head to Shiba. "You've been helpful to her, too, Ms. Shiba."

"Oh, not a problem at all! We happened to have the free space, and Acieth has been such a wonderful conversational partner to me."

With everyone safely in Japan and Emi reunited with Nord, Acieth was, in a way, without anything to do. She had been living as Nord's daughter under the name Tsubasa, but with Nord's real daughter now in the picture, she had to step away from the limelight a little bit. Simply dismissing her would be heartless, but given her incredibly flighty personality, the idea of letting her live alone generated all kinds of concern.

The obvious suggestion was to have her live with Maou, who was still fused with her, but that presented its own glaring problems. Unlike Alas Ramus, Acieth projected herself as a grown woman—having her live in the same apartment with a bunch of men would mean assorted inconveniences for everyone involved. Assuming Urushihara would be back sooner or later, the sheer headcount made Acieth's moving in an unrealistic idea. Suzuno had volunteered to serve as her guardian, but given that she was already Nord's personal bodyguard, they couldn't place too much burden solely upon her shoulders. The debate got a little chaotic, with Maou suggesting she go live with Emi (conveniently forgetting that Acieth couldn't go more than a given distance away from him).

Surprisingly, it was Shiba who provided the breakthrough—by opening her own house up to Acieth. Almost forcing her to come in, more like. "It would only be temporary," she explained, "and besides, I think I'd like to live with her for a while."

That was a week ago, and even by the second day, Acieth was so used to this living situation that she didn't hesitate to call Shiba "Mikitty." It seemed to be going well, in other words.

"Bell packed up your belongings well enough," Nord told her as they filed into Room 101, "but check to make sure everything's here, if you could."

Despite nobody having any idea Nord and Acieth were in Japan, they had actually found a decent place for themselves. Another one-room apartment like what Villa Rosa sported, with pretty much nothing inside except for furniture, appliances, and clothing, so packing up wasn't exactly an ordeal. Suzuno had done up all of Acieth's belongings, since her fusion with Maou meant the apartment was now out of range.

But—

"Mm?" Suzuno mused, spotting a pained-looking Acieth exiting the apartment with a cardboard box. "What is it?"

"Um," came the reply as Acieth turned upstairs. "Maou, today is the work for him, too, yes?"

"It should be, yes. Are you missing something?"

Acieth took another look through the box—not a particularly large one—and joined hands with Suzuno, giving her an apologetic look. "Yeah, um, sorry. Maybe, I should have told you, Suzuno. Pop, I'm sorry, but can Suzuno pick up something else?"

"Oh, no, I should apologize for overlooking it. What kind of thing?"

"Well, I think Acieth should go herself, shouldn't she?" Shiba gently suggested. "It wouldn't do to have another mistake, after all."

"Well, yes, Ms. Shiba, but she..."

She can't venture too far away from Maou, is what Suzuno meant to say. She was stopped with a light shake of Shiba's head.

"It shouldn't be a problem. Alas Ramus is still a baby, so I brought her back to where she was, but Acieth shouldn't have any latent force attached to her right now."

"Latent force?" This was a new phrase for Suzuno. "How do you mean?"

"And even if she did, I could always... Oh?"

Shiba looked up, realizing something. Acieth and Suzuno followed her eyes, only to find Emi (carrying Alas Ramus) and a petite woman wearing a beret looking at them.

"Emilia...and Lady Emeralda?!"

Suzuno ran up to the surprise guest, all smiles.

"Hellooo. Sorry it's been so looong." Emeralda removed her beret and nodded her greeting to everyone.

"What a shock. When did you come to Japan?"

"Yesterdaaay. Emi has been kind enough to let me take up space in her resssidence."

"I see. But what brings you here so early in the day?"

"I had a little business I needed to take care of this evening," Emi explained. "But this is lucky! I came early because I was hoping to see Ms. Shiba."

She nodded at the landlord as they approached.

"Good morning, Ms. Shiba," Emeralda began. "I have a request for you."

"Oh, no need to be so formal," Shiba said as she patted down her dress, keeping it from sparkling too much in the sun. "Another visitor from Ente Isla, then? I have a feeling this is not our first meeting, either."

Emeralda bowed deeply at Shiba, beret held to her chest. "My name is Emeralda Etuva. I am indeed from Ente Isla, as you guessed, and I caught sight of you during the furor over on my world, albeit only from afar."

She brought her head back up, eyes sharpened. Her usual easy-breezy atmosphere was a thing of the past as she returned Shiba's withering gaze.

"You appear to be a very strong person indeed," Shiba replied, her voice lowering—perhaps sensing something from her. "As strong as Ms. Kamazuki...or stronger, perhaps. So, what sort of request is this?"

"I came here because I wanted to request an invitation to the 'discussion' to be held three days from now."

"Ummhh..."

Alas Ramus squirmed in Emi's arms a bit. Emeralda looked down at her. "I had heard from Emilia," she continued. "You offered to discuss the 'composition of the world' with her—the Sephirah, and Sephirot, and other things only described in legend within our scripture. I was hoping I could be part of that discussion."

"If you don't mind my asking, what for?"

There was a shade of caution to Shiba's voice. There was not a hint of wavering to Emeralda's.

"So we can bear it together."

She looked at Alas Ramus and Emi, then Suzuno, before turning back toward Shiba.

"I want to know the same things that Emilia and Bell know, so I can shoulder the weight of our world's upcoming destiny from the start with them." She gave another look toward Alas Ramus. "Once upon a time, Ente Isla took a weight the whole world should have borne and placed it upon Emilia's shoulders alone. Then, without removing it, they tried to simply throw her away. I cannot allow that to happen again. She is journeying once more to discover the truth behind the world, and I am here today because I want to support her—for real, this time. Perhaps I may not look it, but I am among the highest ranks of society in Ente Isla. If the truth Emilia learns is something the entire world must bear, I am in a position to make that known to the people. A position where I can have our populace think about the consequences. So..."

It was an impassioned argument, one few on the scene knew Emeralda was capable of. Shiba nodded on regular occasions as she took it in.

"I understand how you feel," she said, smiling and letting her guard down with a nod. "I suppose Ms. Yusa and Ms. Kamazuki are also from your world. You being with us as well would pose no issue at all. I can tell you are not the type of person to use our discussion for nefarious means. You are free to join Ms. Yusa if your time allows it."

"...My thanks to you," Emeralda replied with another deep bow.

"Uh, so happily ever after?" Acieth interrupted, knowing the conversation was over but having no idea what it meant. The timing made everyone laugh.

"Quite a crowd here!"

"Oh, good morning, Father."

"Morning, Emilia. Who's that?" Nord asked.

"Oh, I haven't introduced you yet?"

"Well, he was unconscious last time, sooo..."

The tension now a thing of the past and her accent back to normal, Emeralda turned to Nord and gave another bow.

Emi took another look around Room 101 of Villa Rosa.

It was naturally similar in design to Room 201 above, but it was funny how the view out the window could change the entire feel of an apartment. There wasn't much to move, so most of the boxes had already been emptied, the place already looking like it had been lived in for several days.

"I'm sorry to put you through all this for my father's sake," Emi said as she bowed apologetically to Suzuno. "I should really be doing some of this myself."

Suzuno shook her head in reply. "I have a great deal of free time on my hands. Do not worry about it."

"A planetarium?"

Emi and Suzuno looked up at Nord's exclamation.

"Oh, yes, I *did* buy something like that, didn't I? Did we put it in a box somewhere?"

"Mm, it was treasure to me, so I hid in place where it is hard to find, yes? I think that is reason why Pop and Suzuno did not see it."

"Can you really hide a planetarium?" Emi said, miming one with her hands. "I mean, they're pretty big, aren't they?"

"What is this planetarrrrium?" Emeralda asked, curious.

"It's this thing that lets you see the stars. Well, not exactly, but... Mmm, how should I explain it?"

"See the starrrs? So like a telescooope?"

"No, not directly looking at the stars, but...like...how to put it...?"

"Perhaps the term 'celestial theater' would be more familiar for you?" Suzuno offered. "I am fairly sure someone in your position would have used one before."

"Ohhhh, I seeee. A tool that lets you plot the paths of the starrrs?"

"That sounds like an even more complex way of putting it," Emi commented.

Suzuno ignored her. "The general purpose of it is the same, but in Japan, a 'planetarium' generally refers to a place where virtual stars are optically projected against the walls or roof of a room, allowing people to enjoy viewing them."

"You make it sound so technical..."

"Picture a domed chamber with a black sphere in the center which houses a strong source of light. If you extinguish all light in the chamber and cut a small hole into the sphere, a point of light will project itself against the ceiling of the dome, looking very similar to a star."

"Ooh, I see. Verrry interesting! But is something like that small enough to be eeeasily missed? It sounds like a very larrrge facility."

"No! It super-thin!"

"Super-thin?"

"Perhaps," Suzuno suggested, "she means the type you assemble yourself?"

Nord nodded, finally recalling the exact object. "Yes, she made the planetarium out of thick sheets of paper that she had to fold and assemble in a certain order. I think it was called 'paper'…um…"

"Papercraft?"

"Yes, that. It was included as a bonus with some magazine and Acieth kept bugging me for it, so I wound up purchasing several issues in a row. The first issue came with a pedestal about this size…" He traced a square in the air, around four inches to a side. "And later issues came with new sheets of papercraft and a guide to viewing the stars for this or that season of the year."

"Oh, yeah," Emi said, "you see ads for that on TV every now and then. Or, like, for a series of magazines that come with individual sets of parts, and if you put them all together, you can build a model sports car or whatever."

Acieth eagerly nodded. "But," she added, "there are lots and lots of sheets, so if you leave unassembled, the dust covers all of it, and very dirty. So I take apart the ones I like, I put them in folder, and I hide them under the baseboard in closet. So I open the box, I see only pedestal, and I think 'Oh no, I forget!'"

"Under the baseboard, eh?" Nord brought a hand to his forehead. "Yeah, I didn't check it that carefully. That piece belongs to the apartment anyway."

"I put it under newspaper in there, too. For extra safe!"

Whether it was a proper place to keep those paper sheets safe or not, it indicated that Acieth treated them as rather precious.

"So Acieth can't travel a certain distance away from him?" Nord said, slowly standing up. "Ah, well. I suppose I'll go, then. I'm sorry, Bell, but would you mind joining me?"

✳

"These traaains go so faaast! Woooo!"

"Eme, try not to scream and carry on in the train, too, all right?"

"I'm nooot! Wooo!"

Emeralda smiled a little at the caution, even as she kept kneeling on her train seat, face plastered against the window as she stared at the scenery rolling by.

"Can you blame her?" Suzuno wistfully said. "When I first traveled by train, I was just as surprised by the speed, among other things."

"Sorry to make you all do this for Acieth's sake," Nord said from his seat next to Suzuno.

To reach Nord and Acieth's old residence, they had to travel around twenty minutes from Sasazuka, get off at Chofu Station, then take a bus another twenty minutes to a stop near Tokyo's main astronomical observatory. It took an hour or so, if they were lucky with the bus transfer, and ever since returning from Ente Isla, Nord had had Suzuno with him for each trip. The chances of any real danger were slim, but they could never be too careful.

With Emeralda paying a rare visit to Japan and Emi expressing a desire to retrace her father's steps around the greater Tokyo area one more time, they had decided to fetch Acieth's forgotten belongings as a rather large group.

"Ooh," Emeralda said, still glued to the window, "but why did you decide to liiive where we are going, Norrrd? You had come to Japan a lot earrrlier than Emilia did, riiight?"

"Oh, you haven't heard about that yet, Emeralda?" Suzuno said, turning toward her.

"No. I was hoping for the chaaance to ask Emilia yesterdaaay…but do you think you could tell meee?"

"You could've asked anytime. I don't mind. It just makes me

think, though—maybe my father and I walked right past each other sometime, in Tokyo, and we never even noticed."

Emi looked at Nord. He winced, as if an old war injury was acting up again.

"Indeed," he said, "and it makes me wonder why Satan and all these top-level demons decided to set up in Sasazuka, too. But it also has a little bit to do with the reason why Emilia isn't letting me help her repay her debt to the Devil King."

Emi scowled at the observation as Nord focused his eyes a little and began to tell the tale.

—I actually first came to Japan not terribly long ago. No more than several months apart from when Emilia and the Devil King arrived, I think.

Since giving up young Emilia to that squadron of Church bishops, I attempted to fight alongside our royal forces and the other villagers to keep our home safe from Lucifer's army. My wife had already left me a Yesod fragment by that time, and while I wasn't perfect at it, I learned how to manifest it into a sword. I was a simple farmer, without any formal magic training, so I was hardly able to extract much force from it. But it still gave me the resolve I needed to risk life and limb to keep my village, my fields, away from harm. I had promised Emilia and my wife that we would all live together again.

But as you now know, such a hastily prepared holy sword was no match for any demon in the Devil King's Army. I was routed from the village, along with many of my fellow villagers. And I hate to admit it, but I doubt there were even ten demons among the force Lucifer sent to conquer us.

I spent the next two years wandering the land as a war refugee. I imagine you know this, Emeralda, but communications across most of the continent had all but crumbled. My understanding was that there was little point sending a message to Saint Aile or the Church, since it was guaranteed never to reach them.

After being routed from our village, I often lacked even the money for some paper and a pen. I wasn't even able to inform Emilia, whom I assumed was in Sankt Ignoreido, that I was safe. Whenever I did send a letter, once every few months, it never amounted to anything—either it was lost on the way, or the Church was deliberately hiding them from her. It makes sense. If she ever did receive one, she would have known I was alive long ago.

So time passed, and soon Lucifer's forces advanced into the imperial capital of Saint Aile. I lived for two years under his army's rule—in other words, for as long as that city was under demon subjugation, I was living in this or that odd corner, eking out a meager existence. Things only changed after Lucifer fell and Saint Aile was freed once more, but even then, it took a long while for Emilia's name to be known among the refugees and common people. Around the time Castle Ereniem was recaptured, the word on the street was that a Church archbishop and one of his elite knights had defeated Lucifer—the name Emilia didn't begin to spread around until several months later, when the Northern Island was freed.

The news shook me to the heart, the fact that Emilia had grown to be a splendid warrior—the kind of evil-dispelling force my wife had told me she would become. But as just another war refugee, I had no way to reach Emilia as she stormed across the continents, decimating the Devil King's Army. I tried contacting her through the Church several times, but you must keep in mind, she was the hope of an entire people. The hopes and aspirations placed upon the Hero and her team must have been dozens, hundreds of times what, say, the average Japanese person would feel for a sports star or pop diva.

Millions of people, worldwide, were targeting their prayers toward that one small group of warriors. No doubt there were many who pretended to be Emilia's friends or relatives. They treated me as just another one of those swindlers. Bringing up our home village of Sloane had no effect. But even if they recognized me as her true father, at the rate Emilia was bulldozing her way across the land, getting a letter to her would be a fool's errand.

So as I whiled away the time in Saint Aile, word came that Malacoda of the Southern Island had been defeated. Things really began to move around that time, I would say. The local governments removed a lot of the restrictions on travel and commerce that were in place at the time. You started to see major efforts across the continent to rebuild the world economy and strike back against the Devil King's Army. You started to see compensation be paid for war refugees.

And it all made me think: If I can't pursue Emilia, why not just wait at a location I was sure Emilia would be soon?

Luckily, after receiving my compensation, I obtained permission to return to Sloane, and my homestead. The village was in shambles, but the foundations of all the homes were still largely intact, and there was enough remaining that I thought we had a shot at reviving the village once we worked the fields a little.

Did anyone else join me? Sadly, no. I was the only one. There honestly weren't many survivors, and after all the time we spent as refugees, most of us had already built new lives elsewhere. Some refused to go home at all; some lost their lives under Lucifer's rule. Many different stories. And even if others had the will to return home, most of them were forced to rebuild their lives in the nearby walled city of Cassius first.

Looking back, I suppose it was part of Archbishop Olba's plan to bring as many people into Cassius as possible. But by that point, I was fairly well convinced that Emilia would have the Devil King on his knees before long. Once she did, I imagined, she would be bound to return to the village.

But the person who did arrive at Sloane after a few days was completely beyond my expectations. In a way, it was an even greater shock than if Emilia had returned. Instead of her...it was Laila, the woman who gave a young Emilia to me and simply disappeared one day, without a trace.

The four of them filed out of the train after it arrived at the platform in Chofu. Taking the long escalator to ground level, they found a large bus depot on the right.

"When I first came here," Nord commented, "the main Chofu

station building was still aboveground. It's changed quite a bit in such a short time. Ah, it'll be that one," he added, taking the lead and lining up at a certain bus stop. The map on the pole, marked BU-91, showed OBSERVATORY as one of the stops.

"This is the bus you want for reaching the observatory station, but on the way back, it's sometimes faster to disboard at Chofu-Ginza, one stop ahead, and walk from there. The intersection on the other end can get jammed pretty easily."

It was rather odd to have a visitor from another planet give a guided tour of the western Tokyo suburb of Chofu—ironic, in fact, given how nobody in the group was native to this particular world.

"When I first came to Japan, I lived in Shinjuku for a short while."

"You were that close to us…?"

Suzuno had already heard this, but even now, it made her groan a little. Nord and Emi had been living a little over twenty minutes away from each other by train, totally oblivious to the other's presence, as they lived solitary lives in Tokyo for nearly a year.

"Indeed. And after a while, Acieth sort of manifested herself. She was never a baby like Alas Ramus; she looked like she does now from the very beginning. She kept whining about how she wanted to live someplace where she could see the stars. So I asked the man who helped us get on our feet in Japan, and he suggested this town, with the observatory."

As he put it, the man's name was Sato, a family name that Nord himself borrowed and used as necessary. But that raised the question of what he did before this Sato gentleman showed up. Emi, along with Maou and Ashiya, had to work hard to assimilate to this new world, but being able to use their demonic or holy energy to overcome the language barrier was a huge help. Meanwhile Nord, a common farmer, had to climb that barrier and build a livelihood for himself alone. How?

"Oh that? That was simple," he said as he boarded the arriving bus, picked up a transfer slip, and headed for the rear seats. "My wife had taught me the basics of Japanese."

*　*　*

—As I toiled in the fields, chopping down the overgrowth in an attempt to revive our ruined village, Laila came down to visit me. And before I even had a moment to doubt my eyes, she spoke to me. She said, "I had no intention of inviting all this upon you."

I had no idea what she meant, but before I could ask, she continued. "We must make your holy sword grow, become more mature, just in case. We must hurry to the land of our memories." By "holy sword," she meant Acieth as you see her now, but at the time it was merely this rather odd sort of sword I happened to possess.

There, underneath the setting sun, I followed Laila's directions to manifest the sword and asked her what this was all about. Even as we spoke, Emilia was still fighting the Devil King's Army. I asked if I could use this force to help her, somehow, or if Laila could use her angelic strength to lend the Hero a hand.

Laila's reply was just as unexpected as always. "I don't know why any of this has happened," she said. "Satan was a gentle child. He knew what it meant to bear pain in one's heart." It made no sense to me. Satan was the name of the very Devil King trying to conquer Ente Isla, and now Laila was speaking as if she knew him personally.

"I apologize for putting all this burden upon you," she told me, though. "I will tell you everything I can right now, so please, let us go to the place of our memories."

So, still not knowing anything, I was taken by the hand as Laila flew us to a mountain east of Sloane. It was normally half a day's journey from the village; it is a hunting ground now, but when we lived there, it was just a regular mountain, mostly untouched by human hands. About halfway up the southern side, we came across an outcropping of flat terrain, like a terrace. Laila and I enjoyed spending time there, when we were young, and I had built a small cabin up there for us to enjoy when there was no field work to be done. To tell you the truth, it was like our secret chalet, just for the two of us. And it was there, in that place from our memories, that Laila invited me.

...Emilia, why do you always act so peeved whenever I bring up this mountain? We liked to call it the "Terrace of the Stars." ...Why all the alarm, Emeralda? Is it that strange of a name?

When we arrived, Laila separated my body from my Yesod fragment. It was a small fragment, easily fitting in the palm of her hand, and she buried it in the terrace grounds, in a corner that received the first of the morning sun each day. I still don't know what she did that for—or should I say, she told me, but I couldn't fully understand it.

Once she was done, Laila and I talked about all kinds of things. The meaning of the Yesod fragments granted to myself and the newborn Emilia. The truth behind the angels, the Sephirah, and the tree of Sephirot sung about in our scriptures. The story behind Satan, the leader of the Devil King's Army threatening all of Ente Isla. The legend of the great disaster engineered by the other Satan, the Devil Overlord—a topic even now deemed taboo among the heavenly realms. It was nothing I had any chance of understanding all at once.

Laila herself was almost in a panic. I believed in her, but before I could fully digest everything she told me, she said that she had a language she wanted to teach me—Japanese.

...That's right, Emeralda. It means that Laila was already fully aware of this world by that point. I suppose that, from a fairly early time, Laila was planning to evacuate us from any heavenly threat... or evacuate our Yesod fragments, I suppose. It was a plan she had been carrying out over a long period of time.

At the time, I was far more concerned about what would happen to Emilia, fighting for Ente Isla, than the goings-on of some world I had never heard of before. But Laila said she would stake her very life on keeping Emilia safe, and I believed her. So I followed her instructions.

Hmm? Why was I so willing to believe in her? Well, how can I put it? It's not easy to explain. Thanks in part to the way we met, I knew from the start that Laila was an angel. Emilia was born after that, and before she left me, well, we had assorted things happen to us.

For example, I knew that Laila bore untold amounts of strength as an angel, but I don't think I ever saw her use any of it, no matter what. We had an extremely cold summer one year, to the point that we knew our harvest would be ruined. So I asked her: Could she use her powers to save the village's wheat crop? And she told me: "If I twisted the path nature takes this year, it is bound to bite back at us later. Do you want to make me into a *real* angel?" That wasn't the only time, either. The way Laila acted often made me wonder if she detested the very fact of who she was.

After that, I resolved in my heart to never rely upon Laila's hidden abilities. Not even a little bit. And it was fine. She always smiled at the used clothing I would pick up from passing merchants. She loved dyeing them in colors provided by the other farmers' wives. Her beautiful skin would crack at the cold of winter, become bruised in the farmwork, get dirtied as she handled the manure. Yet she never hesitated once at any of it.

It wasn't always fun. More than once, we had the kind of arguments that would've led most couples to break up. But never in my life did I ever doubt what lay in her heart. I didn't need to. There wasn't any logic to it. I just believed in her.

Let me talk about the day Emilia was born. It was an incredibly difficult birth. I had no idea that Laila had the ability to let forth such piercing screams from her slight frame. Anything I could do meant nothing more than a stalk of wheat to her.

She'll probably get angry if she finds out I told you this, and she swears she never said it, but both the midwife and I heard it ourselves. Laila, in the throes of labor, shouting out of nowhere: "I hate those sea birds so much, I could die! Flying around in the air, not a care in the world!" It makes no sense, does it? I had never been to the sea in my whole life. There wasn't much I could say in response to that. But it made me laugh nonetheless, and Laila promptly kicked me out of the room.

After a while, I finally heard the cries of our newborn. I ran back inside, and by the time I did, Laila already had Emilia cradled in her arms. I wasn't sure what to say—my voice was just as sobbing as Emilia's own. But Laila turned to me, with her own tearful face. She said, "Thank you." That "I've finally become a human in this world."

It was only until that night at the Terrace of the Stars, fifteen years later, that I finally began to understand what she meant. Fifteen years later, the first time we had met since then, and she spoke to me there. She said that she and the rest of heaven's residents were none of the angels sung about in scripture. We call them "angels" for convenience's sake, she said, but to her, the angels were a pack of thieves, attempting to snatch away the god that should have been born from the rest of us. A criminal gang, robbing Ente Islans of their future, and their god, for their own benefit.

She believed that her being an angel, and her kindred carrying out these kinds of atrocities, was something that deserved nothing less than scorn, not worship. She believed life was truly lived only when rooted on the ground, fully lived within the time allotted to you. But if the angels continued to exist, something would happen, sooner or later, that would spell great suffering for mankind. And as she put it, she had to do whatever it took to prevent that.

But those who wanted to keep Laila muzzled had already taken her away from Emilia and me in the past. It happened on the first autumn after Emilia's birth. That night, Laila was in her angelic form—the same form she took when we'd first met. She had always avoided looking that way around me, but I had no time to ask what she was doing. Instead, she gave Emilia and me two fragments from a purple crystal—Yesod fragments.

"You treated me like a person of this world," she said, "and I want you to have these." I asked what she meant, but she only shook her head. "That child and I," she said, "have the power to repel the 'evil' that will envelop this world someday. Right now, we have to make sure this power remains safe."

Looking back, the "evil" she talked about likely wasn't the Devil King's Army at all. It might have been something far greater, and far more evil.

Then she said, "I can't afford to be captured yet—for your sake, and for the sake of Emilia's future. So, please, let me go for now."

I didn't want her to go, of course. But if Laila had a compelling enough reason to drive her away, I had to let her pursue that. I said that I wanted her back someday, that I'd always be waiting for her. She lowered her head to me, and then she embedded the two crystal fragments into each of our bodies.

"I have asked the fragments to protect you," she told me. "I'm sorry I'm doing all these selfish things, but I promise I will return." And then she left. All I could do was watch as she took flight into the air.

By the time the light she radiated disappeared into the eastern sky, I spotted another beam of light like Laila's from the west, shooting past me, as if pursuing her. Then, something very strange happened: Once the light zoomed its way to the east, that holy sword appeared in my hand, without any warning. It didn't look like anything I could rely on too much, but I immediately knew it was the power of the crystal Laila left me. It was vibrating, as if warning me about the belt of light in the sky.

After the lights disappeared, I returned home to find something floating above Emilia's little hands. It was a cross in the air, like a talisman you were meant to pray to. I suppose it was the original, primitive form that her Better Half took at first. After a few moments, the cross, along with my sword, dissipated into a swarm of light particles and disappeared into our bodies.

I did not feel as if I was entrusted with some great, ponderous mission. I just knew that I had to protect my daughter. I had to keep our home safe, so we could pick up where we left off once Laila finished whatever battle she was fighting and came back. This I swore in my heart.

Laila never did return before the Devil King's Army attacked, but never once did Emilia cry for her missing mother. I think it was because she could feel the power of her crystal within her, covering her heart.

"Oop, there's the observatory."

Spotting the next destination on the digital board at the front of the bus, Nord casually pressed the stop button. Then he turned to Suzuno, sitting next to him.

"Mm? What is it?"

"N-nothing," she replied, clamming up as she stared into space.

"Ugh," Emi added, her face similarly tense and blushing as she turned her head downward.

Emeralda, for her part, was turned around in her front seat, almost grinning as she put both hands to her cheeks. "Nowww," she said, "I know this was a very seeerious story you told us, but... um...I dunnooo..."

She was interrupted by the bus coming to a halt. Nord gave them all a puzzled look as he stood up, tossing the transfer slip and a few coins into the pay box. Suzuno and Emeralda followed, looking awkwardly at each other as Emi tried desperately not to lock eyes with either of them.

"That was really a lot to digessst, mmm."

"Hmm?" Nord said as he got off, unsure what Emeralda meant.

The other three all knew they had to hear that story if they wanted a full understanding of the situation they faced. But the glimpses into the passionate early years of Nord and Laila's relationship he wove into the narrative almost overshadowed the whole thing in their minds.

"Whew," Suzuno sighed, taking a deep breath as she brought a palm to her face. "They certainly had the heater turned up high in there."

"Sooo, what brought you two from the Terrace of the Staaars to Mitakaaa?"

"I had no idea you called it that," Emi muttered, still blushing as Emeralda ventured the question.

Nord nodded at her. "Perhaps we could talk about that during the walk over there? Bell and Emilia have been here several times already, but... This way," he motioned.

—When we met there, for the first time in fifteen years, the first thing Laila wanted to do was hide me, and my crystal, as quickly as possible. Her location of choice was not Ente Isla, but Earth.

She gave me instruction on the language I would need to learn, but we didn't use any textbooks or vocabulary drills. Most of my knowledge was instilled in me by Laila's Idea Link, and after that, I practiced for just a few days. I am still not completely fluent in my choice of words when I speak Japanese exclusively, but I have never had an issue bringing my point across.

Laila explained the big hurry by telling me about Emilia's actions as the Hero, as well as the advance of the Devil King's Army. Her holy sword and Cloth of the Dispeller were born from the same type of Yesod fragment as the one that powered my own sword, and as she put it, the angelic race had picked up on their presence.

She had been depositing fragments to all manner of people across the world up to then, and every time the heavens approached one of their locations, she would use her own fragments to guide the pursuers away from them. This had apparently been going on for centuries, long before I was born, which was quite astounding for me to learn. This time, however, Emilia's power was too strong—too much for her to fully conceal. Thus, as a sort of insurance for when someone smelled out Emilia's holy sword, she wanted me to flee to another world. I think that was the way she put it.

I asked her, of course, what would happen if those pursuers caught her. She simply replied that she would stake her life to protect our daughter.

To me, Laila and Emilia are both irreplaceable pieces of my life. I didn't want her to sacrifice herself like that, but if that was the way she wanted to use her massive stores of power, I was in no position to question her. Besides, I believed in her. I wanted to respect her decision, so I followed it.

It certainly wasn't easy. I had a lot more to learn than merely language skills. Money came before everything, actually. Until I saw an ATM for the first time, I had no idea there was this system where you could access your money anywhere in the world, without having to go through anyone else. The whole idea of paper currency, even, was alien to me—these sorts of promissory notes, no gold or silver or bronze in them, and yet they held more value than any gold coin from my realm. It was a difficult concept to wrap one's head around.

She had already arranged a Japanese passport to prove my identity, as well as a pre-opened bank account. That, really, was the first time I began to feel nervous at all. *What have I gotten myself into?* I thought. She was throwing me into this unknown world far too quickly, and we wound up having our first argument in fifteen years over it. It didn't last for long, of course—in a way, us bickering at each other was such a nostalgic memory that we couldn't really keep it up. Why are you looking at me like that, Emilia? …Ah, right.

So after a few days, Laila dug up the crystal she had buried in the Terrace and infused it into my body once again. This was on the day that Alciel lost to Emilia and retreated from the Eastern Island, or at least that's what Laila told me. She took my hands into hers, and she said, "I wish I had more time to let it be born here." She said, "I'm sorry for doing all of this, but please, I need you to believe in me." I told her that I never mistrusted her for a day in my life.

She smiled that pretty smile of hers—that hadn't changed in fifteen years, either—and looked up at the sky. I looked up as well, and was surprised to find an angel up there—a small man carrying a gigantic scythe. For all I know, he was that streak of light I saw pursuing Laila fifteen years before. He bore the same white wings and hair color as the angel I knew, but his eyes were cold as steel.

And that was the last thing I remember. I lost consciousness immediately afterward. And when I woke up, I was on the floor in an apartment in Shinjuku…more toward the Yoyogi neighborhood, actually, but anyway, I was in Tokyo.

I flew into a panic. Laila had told me what to expect, but the moment I looked outside, I was exposed to all these unfamiliar sights and sounds and smells, attacking me all at once. She had also instructed me on what to do once I arrived, but really, it took me three full days to leave my home. This new world scared me—all these unfamiliar people and so on.

So once my food ran out and I was forced outside, I went into a convenience store and did my first shopping ever on Earth. The kind of bread I could buy there with a 100-yen coin was more delicious than any of the wild-oat loaves I had ever eaten in Ente Isla. I still vividly remember the moment I first sank my teeth into it. *What a world I've been thrown into,* I thought.

I spent the next week exploring the neighborhood around my apartment, learning the day-to-day skills I needed. Once I did, I followed through on what Laila instructed me to do. I went on a walk.

Yoyogi Park was within walking distance of me. She had told me to go walking there every day, smelling the trees and lying down on the ground. That, she said, would help raise and nurture the fragment within me. I only found out what she meant after two months of this, when, one morning, the sword suddenly manifested itself and took the form of a person. And that was the birth of Acieth.

It came as a great surprise to me, of course. Freshly born, and already a teenager, essentially. And what's more, she already had somewhat of a grasp of the Japanese language. She knew I was connected to Laila, so we immediately understood each other.

The thing I remember the most about those days was her appetite. We started going through the money Laila had left for us at double the rate from before she was born. We had a fair amount to work with, but given that I had no idea how long this arrangement would continue, I couldn't afford to waste it all the time. It'd be too late if I waited until my account hit zero.

So I decided to look for work. Thanks to my time spent as a refugee in Saint Aile, I was confident I could cut it in pretty much any job out there. So I began to take on day-labor work, and after a while, I came across this man named Sato. It was Sato who helped me learn that the stamp in my passport was actually a work visa, meaning that if I wanted to, I could take on almost any job in Japan I wanted.

Sato was just a regular Japanese man, but he had a pretty unique personal history that granted him vast knowledge. I learned a great deal about Japan from him.

You're probably wondering why I took his name. That was just so it wouldn't look strange, me living with Acieth and treating her as my daughter. I didn't give a fake name to my work contacts, of course, and my bank account was still under my real one. I just told people to call me that as a sort of nickname. I wasn't a great fan of this, but given the circumstances under which Laila threw me into this world, I felt it safer to avoid bandying around the name Justina as much as possible.

That, and there was also the fact that, between Sato's past and my refugee years, we had a lot in common.

Regardless, Sato and I worked together for a while, and one day I asked if there was somewhere nearby where we could have a good view of the stars. He suggested Mitaka, where the National Astronomical Observatory of Japan is located. It's pretty much the nerve center for Japan's astronomy scene, and they hold events every few months that anyone could participate in if they registered. Sato also gave me a work lead in Mitaka—a place he used to work, that came with a cheap dormitory I could live in. I could even take in the night sky while I worked, he said.

I told Acieth, and she was immediately eager to move. I wasn't sure it was such a great idea to leave the apartment Laila set up for us, but I figured that if she needed to find us, she could follow whatever aura Acieth radiated to track us down.

—So here's where we wound up.

Emeralda looked up at the sign in front of the small building before her, one lined with motorbikes parked in neat rows. It read Sesami Shimbun Newspaper—Sales Office, as Suzuno had to explain to her.

"Wait here one moment," Nord said as he casually opened the sliding door and stepped inside. "I'll have the chief open the door for me."

"So that's what he needed a motorcycle license for," Emi observed. She knew that Maou first spotted Nord and Acieth inside the bus on the way to the driver's license center, and she had been wondering what Nord needed a license for in the first place. The lines of Honta Super Fawn motorbikes in front of the newspaper distribution office told the story for her. There were a few bicycles as well, but motorized transport probably made the delivery work a lot easier—and given how Nord would be zipping around on one of those in the early-morning hours, he certainly would be able to take in the night sky as he worked.

Emi hadn't met one herself, but she knew that some college students were lucky enough to score work scholarships, where newspapers would offer housing and a regular stipend in exchange for delivery duties for the morning and evening editions. Being a paperboy wasn't exactly an easy job, but with the body he built on the farm and the indomitable spirit he honed as a war refugee, it would've been a cinch for Nord.

Although TV and the Internet had dulled their position somewhat, newspapers were still a huge part of Japan's media landscape, and working for one would also give him a deeper grasp of what was going on in the world. Perhaps it gave Nord more of an insight on Earth than what Maou and Ashiya had, given how the library had been their only avenue for information access until Urushihara came along.

After a few moments, they saw Nord step out with a middle-aged man and walk behind the building. This was the head of the office; Emi had said hello to him before. The rear was populated with a number of small apartment buildings, similar to the ones in Villa Rosa Sasazuka, and *Sesami Shimbun* was using one of them as an employee dorm.

"By the waaay, Emilia," Emilia said, curiously taking in the sight of these identical buildings next to each other.

"Mm? What, Eme?"

"I know Nord told us that whole stooory, but it still didn't explain why you aren't asking him for helllp in repaying your debt to the Devil Kiiing."

"Oh, yeah." Emi grinned a little and looked up at the sign in front of the newspaper building. "Well, I didn't really need it. I had a little bit of money to work with in my account, and… Well, call me stubborn, but it's kind of my mother's fault, too."

"Lailaaa's fault?"

"Mm-hmm." Emi sighed and shook her head. "I don't think she's a bad person, but at the very least, she's most of the reason why I, my father, and the Devil King are where we are right now. She's the one who gave Father most of the money he has, you know? And I didn't want to rely on that money. And even beyond that, it's not really right to hit up your parents to repay the debts you racked up, is it?"

"Ahh…"

The explanation made sense to Emeralda. But given the urgency of the situation, it still seemed to her that Emi was being needlessly obstinate.

"Nothing can be done about it, Lady Emeralda. There is never any changing of Emilia's mind when it comes to these matters. You could say that she prefers to clean up her own messes."

"I suppose sooo," Emeralda replied, grinning at Suzuno. "Thaaat certainly hasn't changed at all."

"Thanks for the compliment," countered Emi.

Ten or so minutes later, Nord returned carrying a single file folder with the *Sesami Shimbun* logo on it. It was stuffed full of papercraft sheets.

"She built up quite a hoard, it seems!"

"Why is Acieth so enthralled with stars in the first place?"

"Well, if I had to guess…" Nord gauged the folder as she turned to Suzuno. "Even before Acieth was born, whenever Laila talked about the Yesod fragments, she had a habit of always connecting them to the sky, in one way or the other. Her instructions to go walking in Yoyogi Park, for example, and the way she buried the fragment in the Terrace of the Stars so it'd be exposed to light first thing in the morning. To them, the sky—at night in particular—must have some particularly important meaning. And I think…"

He took a thin sheet of paper out from the folder. This wasn't a papercraft starfield, but rather a round piece of clear cellophane placed over a flat sheet of cardboard.

"I think we received this when we went to a moon-viewing event at the observatory. If you place this between you and the moon, it'll project a map of the moon's surface on the wall behind you. Acieth really liked this piece. A lot of her collection is related to the moon in one way or the other."

"The moon…?"

In the holy scriptures of the Church, the moon was a celestial body controlled by the Yesod, the jewel of the world tree. It gave Suzuno something to think about as she observed the folder.

"Good thing you found her collectionnn, though."

"Indeed," Nord said with a nod, "but it certainly didn't take much work. I'd like to discuss a few more things with you all, but there are some issues I have yet to talk to Emilia about. If possible, I'd like to have everyone together so I can fully go through everything."

"Fair enough," Emi said. "I hate to admit it, but we'll want the demons to be present for some of this, too… How about we just bring that back to Acieth? By the time we get back to Sasazuka, it'll be about time for my evening errand, too."

"Oh, speaking of which, Emilia…"

Emi, already walking toward the bus stop, halted at Suzuno's call.

"What is that errand you speak of, anyway?"

"Well…" She grinned a bit, embarrassed, as she turned around. "It's a job interview."

✳

The moment Chiho caught sight of Maou in the break room at the MgRonald near Hatagaya station, she marched right up to him in a huff.

"Maou! I heard the news from Suzuno!"

"Mm? Wh-what?"

The act from this teenager was enough to make Satan, king of demons, his full powers restored to him, edge backward until his rear end was touching the wall.

"I mean, I know you and Yusa are still enemies and everything! But could you at least *try* to empathize with her a little?"

"Oh, um, Chi, that's, uh…"

"I know you've been through a whole lot, and I know that money issues matter a lot to you guys! But I really don't think you should've done that kind of thing! In front of Yusa's father and everything!"

She seemed honestly angry to Maou. "That kind of thing," he assumed, referred to his demand for repayment. He cursed Suzuno in his mind for blabbing to Chiho as he searched for a way to soothe her.

"Well, Chi, I mean... I can explain—"

"Did it ever occur to you that you could've done that someplace where her father wasn't around, at least? Like, your place, or Suzuno's place, or the MgRonald, even?!"

"Please, Chi, let me talk! I had a really good reason for this!" Maou placed his hands on Chiho's shoulders, just in case she decided to grab him by the collar and perform a judo throw. "I don't know what Suzuno told you, but I knew what I was doing, all right?"

"Well, what were you doing, then? Because I heard you made things really awkward between Yusa and her dad afterward!"

That much, Maou didn't need Suzuno or Chiho to tell him. After all, in Nord's eyes, his own daughter was in debt to the nemesis of the entire human race. He didn't seem to see the demon races as pure evil—thanks to his long-term involvement with the Yesod fragments, probably—but even he could tell this wasn't a good position for Emi to be in. And she wanted to repay him all by herself, too. Even with how much higher her take-home pay was than Maou's, paying such a princely sum all at once would likely put a pretty big dent in her savings.

"I... You know, I thought she'd fight back more, is all."

"Fight back?" Chiho raised an eyebrow at Maou's suddenly subdued voice.

"We're talking three hundred and fifty thousand yen, you know? Even for someone working on salary, that's not the kind of money you'd plunk down on a moment's notice, right? Plus, she's unemployed."

"Well, yeah! So, again, why'd you bring that up in front of Nord?!"

"So, like, I figured she'd say no, and then I could suggest her paying me back with her body instead of with money, and... Um, Chi? Chi?"

As he spoke, Maou could literally see the flames burning in Chiho's eyes, her brows arched upward in rage. It was only then that he realized his choice of words was somewhat ill-advised.

"With, with, with, with her *body*...?! Maou! What are you even saying?! That's disgusting! I am so disappointed in you!"

"Chi, Chi, Chi!" Maou flailed his hands in the air. "Please, calm down! I didn't mean it like that, I didn't mean it like that! I meant *this*!" In a panic, he rushed to his storage locker and took out a thin magazine. "I mean, c'mon, this is Emi we're talking about! Her owing me probably pissed her off enough already—if I asked for that much money from her, I figured she'd blow her top, y'know? So I was gonna take this out and suggest it to her instead!"

Chiho, face reddened with anger, took a look at the cover of the magazine, along with the sticky note attached to it. Now she began to understand.

"Maou, you weren't really..."

"I figured she'd be like 'I'm *never* gonna pay that to you! I know I owe you, but that's just way too much!' So if she said that... I mean, I *knew* she was gonna say it, but if she said that, I figured she could pay me back another way."

Maou sheepishly handed her the magazine.

"Like, 'Hey, I know you're jobless right now, so...'"

Chiho accepted it, not sure which way to react. The cover read CITY WORKING—FREE HELP-WANTED MAGAZINE—FOR SHINJUKU, KEIO, AND ODAKYU RAIL LINE NEIGHBORHOODS, a little cartoon pig carrying a sign reading SPECIAL RESTAURANT EDITION! in the middle.

These magazines came with a sticky bookmark attached to an inside page. Opening to it, Chiho found pretty much what she expected.

MGRONALD HATAGAYA STATION IS EXPANDING! NEW CREW-MEMBERS WANTED! NO EXPERIENCE REQUIRED!

She looked at the page, then at Maou, in a daze.

"M-Maou..."

"Like, if you can't pay me back in money, then work for it a little, is what I thought I'd say. But... um, I guess I misread her?"

"..."

He shrugged as Chiho wordlessly handed the magazine back to him.

"Maou?"

"Mm?"

"That's just *mean!*"

The blunt review of his approach stabbed its way into Maou's heart.

"Well, I mean—"

"You mean what?! What were you even thinking?! You could have just said that at the start, if that's what you wanted! Why'd you have to go all roundabout with it?!"

"Well, like, we both have our own viewpoints on each other, so—"

"Can you keep yourself fed on viewpoints? Can you find decent work with a viewpoint?!"

"I mean... No, but... C'mon, this is Emi we're talking about—"

"If you can't be half-serious for a moment and just come out with it, then she's not gonna listen to what you really mean!"

The sheer force of Chiho's tirade had beaten down Maou to the point that he was now seated on a folding chair, facing up to the torrent.

"Who do you think you are, anyway? You aren't some eight-year-old child! If you want to show a woman some kindness, then why were you so mean to her? Who cares if you thought it'd make you look uncool or whatever? For a Devil King, that's just *shameful,* don't you think?"

"H-hang on, Chi. I thought this out, I swear. We really do need more staff around here, and I guess she's pretty nice to people if they're not demons. With her call-center experience, I figured she'd get used to taking delivery orders super quick. That's all! I wasn't trying to be nice to her or...um..."

It was an escape valve, Maou knew, and it proved worthless.

"It's the same thing! Why didn't you just tell her that at the start?! Why couldn't you just give it to her straight that we need crewmembers and you thought she'd be a good fit or whatever?!"

"Well, like… Why? …Um…"

Maou thought he had it worked out. Chiho was rapidly teaching him otherwise.

"Oh, it doesn't even matter anyway! If you thought it'd be all awkward to show a single decent thought for Yusa, you could've at least phrased it as being concerned for Alas Ramus or whatever! Why'd you have to paint yourself as the bad guy from the start instead?"

"You… You know… I'm the Devil King, she's the Hero…"

"Whenever you two get all snippy with each other, has it *ever* resulted in anything good?!"

It was the biggest lightning bolt of the day, and it landed squarely upon Maou's head. He cowered in his folding chair, gingerly looking up at Chiho. Her eyes danced with enough seething anger to give even Emi at her maddest a run for her money.

"This isn't the time to be dwelling on stuff like that! All you guys fought against the angels together in Ente Isla—you, and Yusa, and Acieth and Ashiya, too! Were you thinking about Devil King and Hero crap back there, too?!"

"N-no, I… Nothing like that, no. Suzuno was kinda going on about it a little, but…"

The whole lot of them had already given Chiho a rundown of the events that occurred in, around, and above Efzahan's capital of Heavensky. Hearing about Emi's incarceration in Ente Isla made her infuriated at Olba and the heavens; hearing about Maou's chance encounter with Albert surprised her; the letter Ashiya sent Emi made her laugh; Suzuno's rescue of Emeralda filled her with admiration; and the retelling of Emi's first encounter with Nord filled her eyes with tears all over again. It was a real roller coaster of emotion, and after all that:

"I thought you and Yusa were finally getting along a little more now, too…"

"Chi…?"

Maou was flustered at the sudden twinge of sadness to her voice.

"Maou?"

"Y-yeah?"

"If Yusa really pays that money back to you, and then she starts seriously thinking about fighting you again, what'll you do then?"

"Huh? I really don't think that'll happen, Chi. Not with Alas Ramus and all."

The thought had crossed Maou's mind. Once this was wrapped up and Emi no longer owed anything to Maou, that brought them back to square one. Maou had still not given up on his tyrant-like aspirations, and those aspirations had put Emi and Nord through hell in the past. They were together now, but considering everything Emi had lost, she had every right to demand repayment from Maou, not the other way around.

"I mean…what, is she gonna demand my money or my life? Like, reparations?"

"Ughh!!"

Chiho turned her back to him, repulsed by his obsession with money.

"Look, Chi, I'm sorry! I guess I wasn't really thinking—"

"What does apologizing to *me* accomplish?"

"Ngh…"

Chiho sighed. "You know, sometimes I just don't understand."

"About what?"

"Yusa used to go on about how you were the villain, the enemy, and she had to kill you and everything."

"Yeah. Sure."

"What about you?"

"Hmm?"

"Like, really, Maou, what do you think of her?"

"What do I think? Um…"

This sent Maou reeling. It was odd, but he felt like he had been in this position just a bit ago, albeit with someone else.

"Do you still want to kill her, in the end? Because she's your enemy?"

"Well, no, I'm not going that far, but…"

The sudden leap in Chiho's questioning threw Maou yet again. He knew his answer wasn't much of an answer.

"So you don't? She's a Demon General in the New Devil King's Army, remember."

"Y-yeah…"

Between Chiho and Suzuno, a lot of people in Maou's life were using their Great Demon General titles to lay it on him lately. "Just desserts" didn't even begin to describe it. He had nothing to counter with.

"So stop being so mean and act like the king you are. Show Yusa a new world for a change. Something she hasn't seen yet. Because otherwise…"

Maou sat silently before Chiho's sad voice.

"…I just feel so bad for Alas Ramus."

All he could do was watch as she left for the front counter.

"Marko?"

"Y-yes! I apologize! I put my foot in my mouth in front of Chi again!"

The moment he stepped into the restaurant space, Mayumi Kisaki, manager at the Hatagaya MgRonald and a woman even the King of All Demons had to bow his head to, approached him in even more of a huff than Chiho a moment ago.

"Oh?"

"…Yeah…"

"Marko, I know I don't need to tell you this, but we're not really in a position to be picky with our part-time job applicants. Do you understand me?"

"I…do, yes," he stammered out, breaking into a cold sweat.

"We need to get people in here, and we need them trained before we go all-in on the delivery service. And if I have veterans like you bringing everyone down in the crew, that's gonna affect that process. Right?"

"Rrrr...right, yes."

Every enunciated syllable of Kisaki's speech seemed imbued with ghastly amounts of demonic force. It made Maou's heart shrink inside his rib cage.

As the calendar shifted deeper into fall, the shifts at the Hatagaya MgRonald had begun to come a bit apart at the seams. They had more people on the floor, given that the MgCafé space required more specialization than the rest of the crew positions, but being unexpectedly chosen for the company's pilot delivery program made it likely their current staff wouldn't be enough to keep the place running.

Autumn also meant they couldn't rely on college students to beef up their ranks. Juniors would need to start the job-recruitment process, and that meant they wouldn't be regulars on the shift schedule any longer. With summer vacation wrapped up, the freshmen and sophomores would be busy with new classes. Housewives and the like formed their most stable employee pool, but while they could keep regular schedules, they were often rather inflexible with taking other shifts—and high schoolers like Chiho would have exams to worry about shortly.

This meant that young-adult part-timers like Maou would form MgRonald's vanguard force, but compared to the armies of students, there just weren't that many of them. They needed time, and staff, to keep the place running while they brought on and trained new hires. Otherwise they'd have trouble keeping the current restaurant running, much less all the new delivery business. In any normal time period, Kisaki could use her keen management, her astonishing personal connections, and her own physical strength to handle temporary staff shortages, but this sudden decision from the top brass was a bit too much a load for even her to handle.

"As I'm sure you know, we're trying to field as many new, young, female crewmembers as we can. There's going to be a lot of new people around here shortly. So if I catch you having so much as a teeny little spat with Chi and making things awkward around here..."

For the second time since coming to Japan, Maou saw his life passing before his eyes.

"...I'll be sure you see hell for it."

"...!!!!"

There was nothing more to be said. Maou saluted her, back arched straight up.

"Good grief," Kisaki replied, sizing up his unspoken oath of allegiance. "Now, about these new people..."

"Y-yes?"

"I already have three interviews to handle today. They're all scheduled to show up while you're on duty. You're up at the café all day today, Marko, so keep in mind you might be in sight of us. I have one in the AM and two in the PM hours."

"Got it!"

Maou had been regularly handling the MgCafé space on the second floor in recent days. His accreditation as a MgRonald Barista had a lot to do with that, but Chiho, despite having the same title, more often found herself manning the front counter on the first floor instead. There were several reasons for this. In terms of sheer ability, unless things were particularly crowded, Maou could easily run the café space by himself. As a high schooler, Chiho couldn't handle café-counter shifts that ran near the ten-PM closing time upstairs. Plus, as the theory went, it was always better to have young women manning the front counter than men, since it attracted more foot traffic from the rail station.

"Hang on. We don't have any cheesecake in stock?"

"Didn't you see the news? During that time off you took, the factory overseas where they made the cheese for it had some kind of bacterial infection, so we won't get any in for a while."

"Ohhh, I see... I didn't have much time to check the TV around then, so... Wow, no cheesecake, though, huh?"

"No. Bad news for us, since it was so popular, but not much we can do about it. We'll have to make up for it with our other items. Think of it as a chance to sell customers on the rest of the menu."

The weeklong gap had proven to be much larger than Maou expected. Simply by missing out on seven days' worth of shifts, Maou was absent for a change in the sauces applied to certain burgers, and several names unfamiliar to him were now written on the shift board. He was back in the groove now, a few days' worth of shifts under his belt, but failing to be around for the delivery training session was a grave concern to him. He wasn't the only one who skipped that class, of course, but the more prep he could do for the launch, the better.

"When it comes to navigating Gyro-Roofs on poor roads," he said to himself by the upstairs café counter, "or climbing stairs with them, or throwing Molotov cocktails from the driver's seat, I'm your man, but..."

Not many customers were in the space. There was little to do, and that made him dwell on his situation.

"What next, I wonder...?"

He checked the expiration dates on the food in the freezer and wiped the condensation off the appliances surrounding him. But Kisaki already managed this place with aplomb. After thirty minutes, he was back at the counter, idly waiting for customers to show up.

Suddenly, his mind recalled his conversation with Suzuno at their camp in Efzahan. "I think you should tell Emilia. When you are prepared to."

"Whenever you two get all snippy with each other, has it ever resulted in anything good?!"

It hadn't. He didn't need Chiho to remind him. There was no doubt about that. It wasn't that he regretted being hostile with Emi sometimes, but still, she was absolutely right.

Then there was what Emi told him in Heavensky, as the sun rose: "I'm sorry to put all this on you." And Maou wasn't blind enough not to realize that she meant it. It came straight from the heart. She was thanking him, honestly and faithfully, for the past month.

But even with all that:

"...I'm not being fair, am I?"

Long before Suzuno took him to task about it, Maou had sworn to himself that he'd never tell Emi about the background behind his invading Ente Isla. He even remembered the moment he took that oath. It was not long after they reunited in Japan, before Chiho knew the truth about them. Emi had just fallen down the Villa Rosa Sasazuka stairway, all teary-eyed, and then she said: "You took my home, my father's fields, my father's *life*, my peaceful, quiet childhood! Everything! And I'll never forgive you!"

To Maou, still getting used to human society, it was his truth to accept, his blame to shoulder. And, at the same time, it instilled the belief in him that invading Ente Isla still hadn't been a mistake. If they placed his tragedy against Emi's on the scales, he was sure his side would still weigh more—he told Suzuno as much. And as long as that solemn truth still held:

"...What's so bad with how it was before now?"

Emi—Emilia Justina, the Hero—was, is, and always would be the enemy of all demons. Maou—Satan, the Devil King—was, is, and always would be the enemy of Emi and all Ente Islans. Their life in Japan was still a wrestling bout, just one that happened to fall outside the ring. And instead of a wrestling match, assorted circumstances had turned it into more of a coping match. It had become oddly comfortable, he admitted, but somewhere in their hearts, they all knew it was fragile, ripe for being battered down by one major event or another. If *this* was the event, that would be totally understandable.

"That, as your general in the New Devil King's Army, is my advice to you."

"You named her a Demon General yourself, didn't you, Maou?"

"Ughh..."

"I've got a whole new world to show you."

"Man, *what* am I even trying to do? What should I be *trying* to do?"

"Who are you talking to, Maou?"

"Gah!"

All the voices from the past flitting through his mind caused Maou to overlook Chiho, still looking a bit peeved. He jumped, startled.

"Ch-Chi?! Wh-what's up?"

"That's what I wanna know, Maou. What were you just muttering about?"

"Um..."

The anguish must've been noticeable in his voice. He looked around, snapping himself out of it. None of the other café customers seemed to take notice, so he couldn't have been that loud.

"It—it's nothing. But what brings you up here?"

"Oh, just changing out for you. You've got a visitor."

Chiho's expression told Maou that she didn't believe him, as she gestured toward the stairway.

"A visitor...?" He looked up, following Chiho's gaze, only to find someone very unexpected at the door.

"I apologize for interrupting your work, Your Demonic Highness."

It was Shirou Ashiya, sweating large beads of perspiration despite the crisp autumn air, holding a manila folder as he caught his breath.

"Eesh, I never would've thought you were interviewing here for a second," Maou muttered as he poked around the stuff in his locker.

"I sincerely apologize for my intrusion. Time is of the absolute essence, and I found myself unable to twiddle my thumbs any longer. I will explain matters to Ms. Kisaki later..."

"Ah, don't worry about that. I'll do the explaining. Oh, here it is."

From his bag, Maou took out a brand-new flip-screen phone and handed it to Ashiya. This sleek, silver device was Maou's new handset, purchased by Emi and featuring all the modern amenities to replace the ancient Joose'd Mobile phone that was smashed to pieces in Ente Isla. The memory of Emi from that time, along with Chiho's more recent tirade against him, had clouded his mind. He didn't know how Ashiya read his body language, but the Great Demon General accepted the phone with a deep bow.

Ashiya's manila folder contained the contract for the credit card in Maou's name. He had explained to Maou the crisis that was Urushihara on the Internet in an undisclosed location and advised him to cancel the card ASAP.

"I'm gonna get yelled at if I take time off my shift right now to talk with the credit-card company. You can use this phone to keep track of the card account. If you start to see weird crap on it, I'll do the whole procedure then. I'm pretty sure we can freeze the card online if we have to, so you can do that if shit gets real."

"I thank you, my liege."

"You know how to use it?"

Maou was fairly uncertain that Ashiya, about as Luddite as one can be in modern Japan, knew the intricacies of Web-based credit card management.

"I will consult the manual if I need to. I could also ask Bell for assistance, or Ms. Suzuki if I can reach her."

"Suzuno? Yeah, right. Rika Suzuki, though... I'm on AE, not Dokodemo, but hopefully that doesn't matter. I think she's working right now anyway."

"I will work to handle this myself, but given my lack of experience, I believe calling upon them would be better than simply pushing buttons randomly."

"Yeah. Let's just hope Urushihara isn't as stupid as we think he is."

"I have little to no faith in that, my liege."

Maou giggled at the assessment. "Well, we'll work it out. It's not worth freaking out and expending demonic force on."

"Quite so. Regaining that force has made me realize how few situations on Earth it is actually useful for."

Maou was in full agreement with this. When they first arrived in Japan, starting up their lives from practically nothing, there was no telling how many times they had griped about their lack of dark force. With it, they could summon flames instead of pay the gas bill, bring forth great deluges instead of paying the water company, and keep their appliances humming without using up any electricity. But now that they had it back, it was, in a way, useless. You could get all the water you wanted by twisting the tap; turn another knob to activate the gas, and you were guaranteed hot food and a warm evening. All the world's conveniences were at their fingertips as long as they had an outlet to plug into. Now that their basic needs were all fully addressed, there was nothing they wanted for so badly that they were willing to spend precious demonic force to earn it.

So Ashiya happily sent Maou off to work right after they returned from Ente Isla. Maou was ready and raring to go, even though Suzuno giggled and said, "I had a feeling it would be like this," as he walked off. And none of them—Chiho, Emi, or anyone else who knew Maou's identity—thought for a moment that he or Ashiya would use their force to threaten the safety of anyone in Japan, or Earth.

They didn't intend to, of course. Not because they feared Shiba or Amane, but because the concept of "conquering the world" Maou and Ashiya held in their hearts was a far cry from what it used to be.

Thus, despite having more power than ever before, Maou and Ashiya's demonic force was a frozen asset. Literally. They had condensed it into a hefty piece of physical matter, wrapped it in cling film and newspaper, and stored it in the murky archives of their closet. They considered putting it in the refrigerator, like they did with Farfarello's demonic force, but it was too big for that—and they couldn't run the risk of it seeping into the food in there and potentially poisoning Chiho or Alas Ramus. The size of this hunk of demonic energy was such that it took up the entire second level of the closet, neatly making Urushihara's "private space" disappear without his knowledge, but that was another story.

Slipping the phone into his pocket, Ashiya gave Maou another polite bow. "I must be off, then. You may devote yourself fully to your duties once more."

"Thanks."

He stepped toward the break-room door, then stopped. "Ah, yes. Your Demonic Highness?"

"Mm?" Maou said, turning toward him as he put his bag back in the locker.

"I am not aware of what has happened, but I do you hope you will make up with Ms. Sasaki before long."

"Huhh?!"

He wound up dropping the bag on the floor.

"H-how did you…?"

"It is clear as day, my liege. Ms. Sasaki is a sort of lifeline for us in Japan, and keeping her happy is largely your responsibility. I hope you will be more cognizant of that in the future. Excuse me."

"…"

Ashiya gave him another nod and walked out the door before Maou could respond. He could hear him apologizing to Kisaki or someone on the other side: "Oh…during this busy time…apologize for…regular duties." It wasn't until well after the voice had faded away that Maou put himself back together enough to pick up his bag.

"Uggghhhhh…" He crouched down on the floor, hands to his face. "Ahh, I can't do this. Come on. Get yourself together." He rapped his head a few times as he gathered his breath. "What am I even doing?"

"What *are* you even doing?"

"Uh?"

His subordinate had just taught him how immature, how naïve, how generally careless he was being, and now Kisaki had just borne witness to his self-pity.

"Is it that bad at home right now?"

"Oh, um, no, not exactly…"

It was, to some extent.

"All right. Back to work, then. It's starting to get busy up there. I'll leave Chi up there, so you two work together for now. Okay?"

"Erm."

She closed the door, not waiting for a reply. Maou stood there, silent, for a moment before muttering, "…Mngh!" and then slapping his hands against his cheeks, recomposing himself. "Just gotta handle what's in front of me first!"

He ran up the stairs, only to find several people in line at the counter.

"Sorry to keep you."

"Sure thing!"

Chiho was still keeping up with the orders, but the line began to operate far more smoothly once Maou took position.

"We're almost out of hazelnut syrup, Sasaki," Maou said after taking the last order in line and pouring out three others at once. "Can you get some more from the back while we have a chance?"

"You got it!"

Chiho ran down to the basement storehouse and brought back some syrup from the café menu. The place usually saw a slight bump in the afternoon, but the two of them worked as an efficient team, showing no sign of the chaos that reigned in the morning as they tackled the rush with perfect poise.

It was easy to assume that the café mostly stayed busy between the lunch and dinner rushes, but it also received some prime-time demand from people looking to avoid the lines downstairs, or customers (particularly women) looking for a lighter lunch. It meant that everything from sweets like cake and scones to hardier offerings like hot dogs and sandwiches were flying off the shelves. The MgRonald by Hatagaya station was always busy on the weekdays, but even on weekends like this one, it would often be packed by a mix of families and employees from whichever nearby offices were open. The café's patronage had also begun to tip toward the big crowds on the weekends as of late—and today, as well, the waves of people didn't fully die down until three PM or so.

Once they had a moment to catch their breath, Maou and Chiho found themselves facing each other behind the counter.

"Pretty big rush, huh?"

"You said it," Chiho replied. "I think it was about this busy last week, too, when you weren't here. I handled the afternoon with Ms. Kisaki then, but it sure wasn't easy."

"Huh. If Ms. Kisaki's presence didn't make it any easier, it must've been crazy up here."

During the rushes, Kisaki was capable of handling hundreds of things at once, like some multiarmed goddess, watching over everything going on in the restaurant with more accuracy than a top-of-the-line HD surveillance camera.

"If we plunge right into offering delivery like this, it's gonna be pretty rough."

"I'd say so… Maou?"

Maou turned away from Chiho's upward gaze, nervously adjusting his visor.

"So, um... You know. It might be too late...but next time I see her, I'll try talking to her. Emi, I mean."

"!"

"Just don't expect the world, all right? She used to make seventeen hundred yen an hour, so maybe she'll want to find something along those lines instead. That, and...you know, I said what I said to her, so I wouldn't blame her if she threw me out on my ear, so..."

"That's fine!"

Chiho beamed, totally refreshed from the grueling rush she'd just endured.

"You know... Going forward, I honestly couldn't tell you how the dynamics between Emi and us are gonna play out, so..."

"It's fine!"

"...But I'm just gonna focus on what's in front of me. I guess I'm having trouble picturing the future lately, and stuff."

"You've been through a lot."

"I have, yeah. But, ahh, pondering over the distant future isn't gonna accomplish much. Tomorrow's probably gonna be just as rough, so I figure, let's just tackle that for now."

"...!"

Chiho's eyebrows shot up. Maou's statement must have touched something within her.

"Wh-what?"

"Oh, no, nothing...hee-hee-hee..."

"Okay. But seriously, don't expect a lot, okay? 'Cause I really doubt she'd accept an invite from me!"

"That could very well be the case, yes. But..." Chiho flashed a contented smile. "You put today, and tomorrow, and a bunch of other tomorrows together," she whispered, "and that's the future."

"Mmm?"

"Oh, um, never mind."

Saying that to Maou would just make him worry about a bunch of needless stuff. It might even annoy him. Chiho didn't mean to keep saying it, but she still believed it. If Maou and Emi could keep finding a way, every day, to meet in the middle and work with each other, it'd ultimately lead to a world where the Hero and Devil King wouldn't have to kill each other.

"It'd be neat to see her here, though. I think it'd be fun."

Maou couldn't completely deny Chiho's cheerful assessment. "Yeahhhh, well, it'd certainly be eventful."

"Ooh, but if she does get hired, you'll have to train her, huh?"

The question frankly startled Maou. "Huhhh? Why? There's a ton of other people who could!"

Training a new employee, by and large, meant sticking to them the entire day. Maou had done this for a lot of people by now, Chiho included, but the mere idea of being a mentor to Emi indicated a future filled with all manner of stress.

"Well, I'm not sure you could avoid it, could you? You're the shift supervisor, you've got the most hours out of anyone here, and Kisaki knows you're already acquainted. I think a lot of the staff would remember her as a customer, you know? So I think she'd be your assignment."

It was an accurate analysis, but it made Maou shake his head as he broke into a cold sweat. "No, no, no, forget it," he said. "I didn't even think about training. Just picturing it makes me want to sit in a dark corner. I hope she never comes in here. She'd be better off elsewhere anyway, yeah."

"Oh, come on, Maou!"

"Look, on the slim, *sliiiiiim* chance that Emi actually comes in, then please, Chi, train her for me or something. I'm sure it'd be a lot more stress-free and effective if you were her mentor, not me."

"You know they'd never let me, Maou. It'll be fine! I'll run in if you guys start yelling at each other."

"Oh, see? You're *assuming* we'll start fighting."

"Well, either way, it's a promise, all right? Whether she comes in or not, if she does, I want you to be her instructor, okay?"

"Jesus Christ, this is what I get for trying to be nice to her! I should've made the offer to Suzuno or Nord instead."

"Oh, Maou!"

If Jesus were having lunch at MgRonald, he likely would have been offended to be name-checked by a demon. But before Maou could make any other oaths at Earth-based deities, Kisaki came up from downstairs.

"Marko, got a moment?"

"Oh, sure," he said with a nod as he walked out from the counter.

"Looks like you and Chi patched things up, hmm?"

"It, um, yeah, it's fine," he replied to Kisaki's sarcastic grin.

"All right. I have my first afternoon interview soon, so I'm gonna be offline for a bit. Chi's gonna go back downstairs. We're a little short on staff for the dinner rush, so once I'm done, I'll be back up here. You should take your break pretty soon, 'cause the night shift's gonna be pretty tight."

"All right. Hey, Sasaki, she wants you back downstairs!"

"Okay!" she cheerfully shouted. "Oh, are you gonna be on break soon?"

"Um? I think so, yeah."

"I have the notes I took during the delivery training session, so you can check 'em out in the break room if you want."

"Oh, really?" The offer made Maou's eyes twinkle.

"Sure. I took them for your sake, so..."

While Maou, Suzuno, and Acieth were bounding around Ente Isla for a week, Chiho attended two different MgRonald delivery training sessions. She needed to for work reasons, of course, but she also did it as a favor to Maou, as keen as he was to dive into the new program. It was an offer Maou would never refuse.

"Well, thanks a bunch! I'll check them out later."

"Cool. See you!"

With a satisfied smile, Chiho went downstairs as Maou returned to the café counter in high spirits.

"This relationship makes no sense to me..."

Kisaki, meanwhile, crossed her arms and assessed the pair.

Once he wrapped up his early dinner at four PM, Maou began to gloss over the neatly handwritten notes Chiho had left for him.

"Oh, this is great!" he said to no one in particular as he turned the pages, making sure to wipe the oil from his hands before touching the sheets.

"Oooh…"

From the first page, Maou found himself remarking on how neatly, and colorfully, organized the notes were. He could see Chiho's sincere effort shine through in them, with the important bits marked out with fluorescent marker or red and green pen lines. It even had a couple of illustrations—a quickly sketched portrait of a girl with two pigtails, word balloons provided to give her impressions of this or that point.

Since Chiho didn't have a bike license or a stipend to earn one, most of her instruction revolved around store-side delivery management. It began with the basics of telephone etiquette and moved on to the finer points of delivery packaging and handling the credit-card reader. It also covered which menu items were available fresh for delivery at which time periods, but Chiho devoted the majority of her notes to phone-based customer service. She needed to accurately pick up the customer's name, address, and phone number, check to see if they had any coupons, and provide an estimated time if the place was busy, not to mention the upselling she was expected to do. This she wrote about in great detail, as well as practiced out loud during the training session.

"I think," said one of the pigtailed doodles in the notes, "just memorizing this isn't gonna be enough. You can't see the customer's face, so you have to be even more careful with what you say, or else it'll feel like you're reading a script."

"Good point," Maou said, nodding to the artificial Chiho. The physical presence, or lack thereof, of the customer made counter and phone service two very different things. You couldn't see them, and—another key factor—they couldn't see you. Sticking doggedly to the canned dialogue in the manual would leave the customer feeling cold, like they were talking to a robot.

"So, watch your mouth, I guess. It's gonna be one guy on the phone and another guy delivering it, too, so…"

Even if the order taker provides impeccable service, if the deliveryman acts all sullen around the customer's home, that affects their impression of the restaurant and their food—and vice versa, too. Everyone on the crew would need to redouble their efforts, or else there were some killer traps awaiting them with this delivery system. All the veterans on staff, from Maou and Chiho to their manager Kisaki, were educated enough to instinctively remember and execute that, but right now, with droves of new people getting hired, it was unclear how quickly this could be drilled into the rookies.

"Oh, Marko?"

"Hey, Kawatchi."

Just then, another part-time crewmember walked into the break room, carrying a bag from the bookstore across the street.

"You on break?"

"Yeah. I was just out buying a book."

This was Takafumi Kawata, referred to by both Maou and Kisaki as "Kawatchi." He was large, with rugged, mountain-man looks and a way of speaking that often ventured off the beaten path, but like Maou, he was a jack-of-all-trades, well-trained in every aspect of MgRonald kitchen and floor management. No matter how busy it got during lunch or dinner, people had nothing but praise for Kawatchi's performance, occasionally noting that his burgers "actually look like the ones in the TV ads." Perhaps because of that attention to detail, he was never one to change his pace during peak times, which made him appear to be a slow worker at times—but even then, only in comparison to Maou or Kisaki, who often complimented Kawata on his accuracy and performance.

He was a college student, and apparently a decent one, too, given how he never skipped out on shifts during exam season. He also had his scooter license, and already Kisaki pictured him as one of the keystones of the delivery team.

"Whatcha reading?"

"Oh, um…kind of a résumé, sort of thing? For delivery training."

Maou cocked his head at Kawata's vague response, as Kawata took a peek at the notes in his hand. "Ahh," he said, "so that's what Chi was writing down like mad during the training session."

"Ha! Pretty much. Oh, did you go to the bike training session, too, Kawatchi? Tell me what kinda stuff they had you do."

"..." Kawata thought in silence for a moment before speaking. "Naaah, I'd prefer you stay oblivious."

"Huhh?!"

"Hey, you're the one who skipped out. You deserve to have it blow up in your face two or three times."

"Geez, blow up?!"

As Devil King, Maou was no stranger to the heaps of vilification rained upon him by Emi and the rest of his acquaintances. He never expected similar treatment from one of his own coworkers. He stood up, unsure where Kawata was going with this, but was interrupted.

"Oh, but hey, did you hear about Kota, Marko?" Kawata asked, suddenly serious.

"Mm? No. What's up?"

"Kota" was Kotaro Nakayama, another college student who joined the team a little after Maou and Kawata. They were all roughly the same age, and he was average in terms of work ethic, but between his good looks and generally serious attitude, he could easily be mistaken for some kind of TV personality. Female customers always enjoyed the atmosphere around the counter whenever he was around.

"He said he might quit as soon as the end of December."

"Whoa, really? Why?" This was news to Maou. He stiffened a bit.

"Well, he's a junior in college this year."

Maou took a step back. "Oh. Job hunting, huh?" he muttered, palm against his forehead. "Wait, but what about you, Kawatchi? You and him go to school together, don't you?"

If both Kota and Kawata left at the same time, the impact on the shift schedule would be devastating. The term "job hunting" right now, as twenty-year-olds across the city began to attend company orientations to land the best career possible upon graduation, was scarier to Maou than anything Emilia the Hero could say to him. Just like her, it was an unavoidable enemy to confront.

"Oh, I'm okay on that front."

"You are?"

"Yeah. I'm gonna be taking over the family business once I graduate, so it'll be right back home for me. I'll still be around Tokyo, but…"

"Oh, does your family have a shop or something?"

"Yeah, kind of a small restaurant. I'm probably gonna try to be a professional chef eventually."

"Whoa!" The news was surprising enough to make Maou forget about his own "family" issues. "Is that what you're in school for? Or I guess you'd be in culinary school if it was for that, huh?"

"Well, I'll have to get the official kitchen license sooner or later, but I'm in school for a business degree, actually. It's not a fancy university or anything, but I'm doing research on community management and stuff. I figure it'd be nice if I could use my restaurant to help keep the neighborhood buzzing in the future, you know? It's close to Tokyo, but it's still kind of exurb enough that not a lot of young people stay there, so…"

"Wow… Neat."

Maou wasn't sure how being a chef connected to building the local community. But Kawata wasn't the type to fling buzzwords around to look fancy. He must have believed what he said.

"Kota's all jealous of me, since I have a job lined up and everything. But inheriting the family business is a pretty big leap for me to make, too, so considering what I got waiting for me, I told him we're pretty even, difficulty-wise."

"Oh. So I guess you'll be here for, like, another year at most, then?"

"Yeah, I guess so. I'm kind of freaking out a little."

"Hmm?" It didn't seem to Maou like Kawata had anything to freak out about. But Kawata winced at him and took another look at Chiho's notes.

"Like, with that."

"Oh, the notes? What about them?"

"Not that! Her!"

"Her...?" Maou took a moment to chew on what Kawata meant before turning toward him, lips tensed. "Wait, what? Hang on, Kawatchi, I dunno what you're assuming, but there's nothing between me and her...!"

"Oh, I know, but that just makes it all the more aggravating!"

"Huhh?!" Maou half-shouted.

"Like," Kawata flatly stated, "if you told me you and Chi weren't a thing, then usually nobody would ever believe you, man. I mean, she takes care of that kid from your family sometimes, Marko! It'd be weird if you *didn't* have something going on."

"Oh..."

Kawata was referring to Alas Ramus, not long after she came to Earth and Chiho managed her for a while. He hadn't shown her around or talked about her much to the MgRonald crew after that point, but those harried events were still passed around the break room at the Hatagaya MgRonald, like folklore.

"Wait, Kawatchi, don't change the subject. What are you freaking out about?"

"Oh, I dunno if you'd understand, given how fulfilling *your* personal life is..."

"Wow, way to make me feel special."

"But to me, this is a problem that could affect the whole rest of my life. I still can't get a girlfriend!"

"Wh-what do you mean...?"

"Think about it, Marko. I'm gonna be working in a restaurant where the only other employees are Mom 'n' Dad. You think I'm gonna have any chance encounters in there? If I can't find a girl while I'm still in college, I dunno if I'll ever get married!"

Kawata rapped his freshly purchased book, still in the bag, against the table a couple times to emphasize the point.

"Hmm, yeah, I see what you mean. But you could still, like, go out and stuff, right? You'll have chances."

"...It takes a lot of time, running a place like that. You know that, Marko."

"Yeah…"

Maou, more than a lot of people, knew how difficult it was to be an effective manager. He was, after all, still the supreme leader of what one could technically call a multiethnic kingdom.

"'Cause, I mean, I know I'm here declaring to the world I want a wife and stuff, but it's, like, marriage isn't the finish line, right? It's the starting point."

"Hmm, yeah, true. You're intending to live with her for the rest of your life."

"Right. But, you know, going to a speed-dating event or whatever, you can't tell if the girl you're talking to is really gonna be someone you wanna spend a ton of time with, I don't think. If a girl has all these conditions I have to deal with, that's not gonna be too helpful with us running the restaurant."

Maou nodded at Kawata's frank, oddly calculated evaluation of his love life.

"I really don't think it's that big of a problem, man. Like, I only know you from this job, but it's not like you have zero female friends or anything. You get along with the women here."

"Well, it's weird," Kawata said with a self-effacing grin. "I always seem to hit it off with women who already have guys in their life."

"Ooh…"

Maou was running out of things to say.

"Like, whether it's here, or in class, or at my clubs in college, I know a lot of women, but…yeah. Sometimes I wind up talking to them about the problems they're having with their guys, and they treat me with a meal or whatever as a token of thanks. I mean, I even read a book on how to get a career as a counselor; that's how often it's happened."

"Sure. But… So you're the type of guy that women like to rely on, then. There's gotta be a girl who'll pick up on that, Kawatchi!"

"…Doesn't exactly fill me with joy to hear it from *your* mouth, Marko, but thanks. Man, I wish *I* was adored by a cute girl with big tits…"

"Whoa, watch your mouth!"

During shifts when the MgRonald was staffed by nothing but
men, it wasn't exactly unheard of to hear the occasional sex-
ist remark. But even so, hearing the word "tits" in a conversation
between the serious-minded Kawata and the nonhuman Maou was
a major surprise.

"But, you know, just asking out of curiosity…not out of spite…"

"Sure. You're being weird either way."

"It's that bleedingly obvious to everyone, but you still don't want
to officially be a couple with her? Like, Chi's great. And it's not as if
you don't like her, right?"

Maou didn't need a reminder. He was already perfectly clear on
that point. And while nobody on the crew was around for it, Chiho
had already made her own feelings crystal-clear to him in private. To
him, she was the only human being on Earth that he could wholly
rely on, heart and soul. Suzuno, the only other one around for Chiho's confession, was haranguing him to give her a decent reply to it
already—but not only had he put that reply on hold, he wasn't sure
he could give one at all right now.

He knew he was acting in bad faith toward her. But inside his
mind, he still couldn't reach a conclusion. The more he thought
about it, and how it might wind up changing both of their futures,
the harder it became to find a response.

"Well… I…"

Maou looked down at his notes, ruminating on Kawata's query.

"I guess I'm kind of in the opposite situation from you, Kawatchi."

"The opposite?"

"I mean, not even talking about Chi or anything—the stuff I'm
trying to accomplish, I'm trying not to get other people too involved
in it, I guess."

"Involved? Um, you mean like how you want to get promoted out
of the crew and into a permanent position?"

"Umm, like, stuff beyond that, I mean."

"Oh. Wow, you're thinking pretty far ahead. Wanna own a fran-
chise someday or something?"

"I'm gonna need a lot more money before I start thinking along *those* lines. I don't know anything about management, unlike you. Hell, even three hundred and fifty thousand yen is kind of a vast sum of money in my book."

"Ha-ha! Why three hundred and fifty thousand?"

"Oh, just…came to mind. But anyway, I've got my own dreams, and Chi's just a normal teenager, so I want to keep her out of that as much as I can."

"You do? It doesn't sound like anything that serious to me, but…"

Kawata didn't seem very convinced by Maou's explanation. But he didn't pursue it further. Maou, for his part, felt the conversation had helped some of his depression clear up, although he could never give Kawata the whole story.

He had a way of life, and he didn't want Chiho caught up in it. That was how he truly felt, as long as he kept looking at things a certain way. He was the leader of a kingdom of demons. Even after she learned about that, he had done everything he could to keep her away from danger, even borrowing the skills of his mortal enemy Emi from time to time. But it wasn't enough. Death had been a real possibility for her multiple times.

She knew everything, and she still loved him. But placing her at an even closer position to his life was unthinkable to him. Plus, they had two insurmountable walls between them: a wall between worlds, and a wall between species. The worlds, perhaps they could find some way or another to bridge. But there was nothing to be done about the other wall. Maou was simply unable to mature, and grow old, alongside Chiho. The gap in the aging process between human and demon would catch up with Chiho sooner or later, and he could easily imagine how it could destroy her.

There was just no way Maou could answer, or live up to, her feelings.

"…Hmm?"

But after reaching this conclusion, Maou realized something seemed off with it. He felt something was missing, that he was making too much of a leap in logic. He didn't have time to figure out what it was, though, because—

"Ooh, it's time."

His conversation with Kawata had eaten up most of his break.

"Well, I'm out," he said, placing the notes back in his locker and putting his visor back on.

"Yeah, I'll be joining you in a sec," Kawata said as Maou walked out of the room.

Chiho was still there, at the counter.

"Hey, Chi, I put your notes in my locker for now. You're almost done with your shift, right?"

"Oh, you can take them home if you want. I don't need them right now. You can return them later."

"Yeah? Well, thanks. I'll do that, then."

Upstairs, he ran into Kisaki again.

"You're late. That's almost straight up against the clock-in time."

"I'm sorry," Maou said, a bit tense as he put his time card into the machine. "I got into this long conversation with Kawatchi. He said Kota was quitting?"

"Oh, yeah." Kisaki scowled a bit. "Not much I can do about that, sadly. I can't keep him here on a part-time job forever."

It was now five in the afternoon. Glaring at the time display on the cash-register screen, she put her hands on her hips and took a deep breath, as if steeling herself.

"I'll just have to find someone as talented as Kota. My next interview's at five thirty. Hope it works out." She gave a small, defiant snort. "Funny how these interviews make *me* nervous."

The situation Kisaki faced must have stressed her out at least a little. She had offered no commentary on the first two interviews of the day, and nobody else on the crew felt it proper to ask. They'd know how it turned out in a few days anyway, and all Maou and his team could really do was hope some fresh faces came along.

"Okay, I'm off. You're upstairs for the rest of your shift, Marko, so you'll be taking over from me."

"Got it."

He brought a hand to his visor to salute Kisaki as she left. The dinner rush would commence shortly. Now, he thought, was as good a time as any to give the evening-oriented ingredients another inspection.

Then he spotted Chiho tearing up the stairs, running right past Kisaki. She was in her street clothes, freshly relieved of duty, and she seemed awfully worked up about something.

"M-M-M-M-M-M-M-Ma—!!"

"W-what, Chi?!"

She had almost collided with the upstairs counter, bracing her body against it as she helplessly stammered and pointed a finger at the stairway.

"M-M-Maou, did, did you make a call during your break or something?!"

"Huh? Um, no," he replied, unsure what was triggering this freak-out. "I ate, I looked at your notes, and I was talking with Kawatchi the whole second half of it."

Chiho gave her another pained look. "Really? But then, just now... Huhh? Why? What... Why?"

It was unlike her to get this flustered over something. She held firm, indomitable, against the Sephirot's guardian angel and a high-ranking Malebranche chieftain—if *they* didn't throw her, what could? But something had. Something that occurred just in the few minutes after Kisaki went down for her interview.

"Oh God, did Sariel do something?!"

That was the only thing he could picture—Sariel, the archangel who still managed the Sentucky Fried Chicken across the street from them, was up to no good with Kisaki again.

"Noooooooo! No, not that!"

Chiho shook her head so violently that Maou was afraid it'd twist itself right off. Then she took a glance at the kitchen behind Maou, followed by the customer space.

"Are, are, are, are you doing anything right now? You aren't, right? The customers are all okay!" She grabbed at Maou's arm across the counter, almost dragging him over it. "Just come down! Come down!!"

"Oww! Whoa, Chi! Lemme go! I'm coming!"

Attempting to calm her down before she swung her arm and threw him down the stairwell, Maou checked to make sure no extra customer orders were incoming, then headed downstairs with Chiho.

"H-hurry!"

"Chi, don't look at me, you're gonna fall down the stairs… What *is* it?"

Nothing seemed amiss among the customers on the ground floor. There was no Sariel making an ass of himself; he wasn't there at all. The counter and kitchen area seemed just as serene.

"M-M-Maou! Over there!"

"What? What're you…"

Noticing that Maou wasn't looking where she wanted him to, Chiho tugged at his arm and pointed toward the entrance. He turned to it, bewildered, to find Kisaki talking to someone near it. His manager had her crew cap off, gesturing the person to follow her. The final interviewee, maybe? Kawata was probably still in the break room, so Kisaki would probably conduct it in her private office, in a separate building nearby.

"Mmm?"

"Maou… That person…"

Suddenly, Maou noticed something strange. The mystery person's back was turned, but something about it seemed familiar to him.

"You see, Maou? That has to be it, but…why?"

It was more than simply familiar, in fact. Maou and Chiho knew that rear like the backs of their hands.

Her being at the restaurant wasn't that unnatural. She had made several visits before. But why was she having a personal conversation with Kisaki? Why was she taking her into her office? She wasn't just a customer? She wasn't being expected to make an order and sit at a table somewhere?

"……!!!!"

Maou, unlike Chiho, was at a loss for words. He had no idea what he should even say. His mind was a blank as Chiho kept a shaky hand around her arm.

Suddenly, the woman leaving MgRonald with Kisaki turned

toward them, immediately spotting the two employees staring slack-jawed at her. She flashed a slightly awkward smile, gave a light wave to Chiho (and not Maou), and followed Kisaki out the door.

"E…Emi…"

"Yeah, you see?! That was totally Yusa just now, wasn't it?!"

Emi Yusa, the final interviewee of the day, was just there, right before their eyes.

※

"E-E-E-E-Emi! Youuuu!"

"Wow, that's how you say hello?"

His shift wrapped up, Maou opened the door to Room 201 of Villa Rosa Sasazuka and pointed a finger straight at Emi—who was sitting in the middle of the room, along with Ashiya, Suzuno, and Chiho, like it was her God-given right.

"You…!" he stammered again, suddenly frozen solid at the doorway.

"Welcome home, Your Demonic Highness," Ashiya said, giving Maou a sympathetic look. "I hope your day at work went well. Why don't you come inside for the time being?"

Maou stayed planted where he was, lips trembling.

"It must have been quite the shock," Suzuno observed.

"Oh, it sure was!" Chiho replied. "I almost jumped out of my clothes when I saw her."

"Ch… Um, Chi, like…"

"Yeah? Oh, I got my parents' permission for this." She pointed at the nearby wall. "I'll be staying at Suzuno's place tonight."

"No, I… I mean, yes, that's great, but, uh…there's no more trains now…"

The clock on the wall read half past midnight. Maou got off work at midnight, so reaching home this quickly took a concerted effort on his part—and Emi and Chiho were waiting for him here, as if counting on that. He looked at Emi, then at his own watch.

"I'm staying with my father tonight," Emi casually stated, pointing a finger at the floor.

"Ah, yes. Devil King, I have just given Alciel the remaining unpaid half of your week's salary," Suzuno said. "That only leaves the scooter, which I hope you will decide on soon. And that marks the end of Emilia's monetary repayment, so I do not want to see you attempt to charge her interest on that scooter."

"Uh, sure... Wait. Already?!" Maou put a hand to the wall, almost collapsing at his own doorstep as he looked at Ashiya. His associate meekly showed him a white envelope.

"Are you... Are you sure you can *do* that?! What're you gonna live on this month?!"

Even ignoring the scooter, Maou had asked Emi for over 200,000 yen. Seeing it returned this quickly made him worry about her continued financial health. But Emi simply nodded at her, nonplussed.

"Remember, I made seventeen hundred yen an hour. Plus, I don't waste money on too much stuff. I could pay you right now for a scooter, too, as long as you don't get too fancy."

The calm, composed declaration made Ashiya look honestly impressed. "Such broad-minded confidence!" he exclaimed. "You truly are the detestable Hero we have always known you to be, Emilia."

"*That* makes her a Hero to you?" Maou countered. He took a deep breath, attempting to gather his composure as he removed his shoes and came in, his face tightly wound as he took a seat next to Emi. Seeing this act, Suzuno and Chiho couldn't help but exchange a wry grin.

"What?"

"Don't 'what' me," Maou spat at Emi. "What're you trying to do?"

"What do you mean?"

"I *mean*..." He rapped at the tatami-mat floor, almost pleading at her. "Why did *you* apply to join *my* location?!"

"It's a little late, you know," Emi calmly replied. "You really shouldn't beat on the floor like that. You'll wake up Alas Ramus."

"Whaaaa…?" Maou's face reddened. He tried his best not to explode in front of the serene Hero. The mention of their child's name forced him to place his hand back in his lap.

"Look, I talked to Kisaki!"

"Yes? The manager? What of it?"

"She said she was gonna hire all three of the guys she interviewed today!! You're gonna be—"

"Oh, she did? Wow! Great!" Chiho exclaimed. For whatever reason, she was much more upbeat at the news than Emi. She beamed with joy, leaning over and giving her a hug. "Yusa! We're all gonna be working together! This'll be so fun!"

"Yeah, it'll be nice having you show me the ropes. Thanks in advance for that."

"Such great news, Emilia," Suzuno chimed in, "finding your next occupation so quickly. It certainly puts my mind at ease."

"Yeah, sorry if I made you worry. I'll have to tell Rika and Eme later, too."

"Whoa, whoa, whoa, *guys!*" Chiho's sheer glee made Maou relent a little bit at first. He struggled to regain the initiative. "Wait a second! Let me speak first!"

"About what? We've already talked about everything. I told Bell and Alciel and of *course* Chiho about the story, so go ask one of them later. If Ms. Kisaki really calls me for the job, I'm gonna be working there, all right? So stay out of my way."

"That's what *I* wanted to say!" he argued, although Chiho's doe eyes stabbing into him as she hugged Emi blunted his momentum. "Emi, look, please tell me. What could possibly have driven you to apply for that job? You're gonna be making a whopping eight hundred and fifty yen an hour during your training period, you realize? That's, like, half your old salary. You're okay with that?"

It was true that Maou considered giving Emi a reference for the job, just like he told Chiho—no matter how much he had screwed up the execution. But he never thought Emi would volunteer to apply.

"Ughhh…" Emi sighed as she gently removed Chiho's arms from her body. She gave her and Suzuno an ironic grin—and, seeing the three girls share some unknown, unspoken secret with each other, Maou realized that Ashiya had the exact same grin upon his face as well.

"...Devil King," Emi said. "I know I'm repeating myself, but I really do appreciate what you did for me back there."

"...Huh?" Maou replied, eyes bugging out.

"I apologized a lot to Chiho and Rika. I told Eme and Al, too. I..." She turned her head up and looked around the room, her gentle eyes taking in all of the Devil's Castle here in Room 201. "I really like the meals we all eat in this place."

"..."

"I don't know if you intended it or not, but the way it all turned out, my father, Alas Ramus, and I are pretty much free from anything in Ente Isla that could hold us down. It wasn't easy all the time, but I survived it without abandoning hope for mankind—or demonkind, even. And that's all thanks to you."

"Y-yeah... Well, that... Yeah."

Maou edged back a little from Emi, looking supremely awkward as he kneeled on the floor. He wasn't sure she had ever talked about herself like this to him—and so gently, no less.

"But, you know..." Emi continued, her voice suddenly growing stiffer as she fixated her stern eyes upon Maou. It made him hold his breath a moment. "That's why I can't let myself depend on your goodwill like this. Because, I mean, you really screwed up my and my father's lives, and I'm afraid I just can't let that slide. You're... You're still my enemy, after all."

"Yeahhh, um. Yeah, I guess so," Maou replied, meekly nodding. He used his peripheral vision to size up Suzuno, unsure where this conversation was headed. She hadn't blabbed to her about that fireside "confession," had she? But whether she failed to notice Maou's gaze or simply chose to ignore it, Suzuno did nothing in reply, listening to Emi speak.

"And when you stormed into my father's room to demand payment from me... You never really intended to take this much money from me, did you?"

"Huh?! Ah, um, like… Chiiii?!"

"I didn't say anything," Chiho responded, shaking her head. Just as calm and serious as Suzuno, Maou observed.

"Indeed," Suzuno noted, "your childish antics provided little in the way of camouflage for you from the start."

"Right. You played your stupid game because you were waiting for me to say 'No way, I'll never take that in a million years.' Then, once I did, you'd tell me to get a job over at MgRonald. Am I wrong?"

"Nnnngh… No, it's just…"

"Maou?"

Chiho's voice was sharp, pointed, as Maou continued to search for some kind of excuse.

"Give it up," Suzuno said as she took out the half-wadded up classified magazine from under the table. The sight of it made Maou's eyebrows arch upward. It was a different free publication from the one Maou showed to Chiho at MgRonald; he thought he had tossed it in the trash after his overtures toward Emi had failed.

"Is that…? Geez, Ashiya! I told you to throw that out!"

"I could not, my liege," Ashiya explained, eyes averted. "We had just missed the date for recycling pickup."

"Then burn it!" Maou shouted, shaking Ashiya's shoulders. "This is exactly what our demonic powers are for, man! We can use our dark forces to hide all the evidence!"

"And that, Your Demonic Highness, is exactly why I told you it was best *not* to prod Emilia so much. To leave her be instead. This was your doing, and your responsibility to bear."

"Responsibility…?" Maou turned to Emi, his hands still on Ashiya's shoulders.

Then:

"Wh-*what* the—?!"

With a near-scream, he swiftly retreated to a corner of the room. The moment he turned around, he had been greeted by the back of Emi's head. She was bowing toward him. Emilia, the Hero. Emi Yusa, the woman who hated Maou like nobody else in all the worlds. And now she had her head hung in the air.

"Thanks. For thinking about me."

"Whoa, stop, stop, stop! Are you really Emi?! You aren't Gabriel transformed or something?!"

Maou's body shook, like a rabbit being leered at by some unknown, slavering beast. Emi lifted her head and smiled.

"With what you did, at that battle in Efzahan...you helped my father and me, and our village, slip away from the dark conspiracy threatening all of us. For that, I thank you from the bottom of my heart. Just think of the money and the scooter as a token of my appreciation. No matter why you said that, all right? But like I just said, I still can't forgive what you did. So now that I'm back here, I can't let you consider my feelings any longer. That much, I want to be sure we're clear on."

"......"

She slowly stood up, and Maou tensed his body in dreadful anticipation for what she might do next. Instead she turned to Chiho and Suzuno.

"Well, it's late, so I need to go back to my father's room. Good night, Chiho. And thanks for helping with my father again today, Bell."

"Sure, have a good night!"

"It is my pleasure. I will do what I can to help Nord get used to his new life."

"Thanks. Alciel, Devil King... Sorry to bother you so late."

"...Not at all."

"..."

Nodding at Ashiya, and not bothering to wait for Maou to summon a reply, Emi put on her shoes and left. The sound of the door closing behind her echoed for just a moment, and as if it was a cue, the other three people in the room turned to Maou.

Before he could figure out what they were looking at him for, his body was in motion. He flew out the door, and after Emi. Just as she said, she was staying in the apartment downstairs. There was no great need to rush out at top speed, but somehow, he felt like he had to stop Emi before she closed her door. He spotted her in Villa Rosa Sasazuka's front yard—or, really, she was looking up at him frozen, perhaps realizing he wouldn't want to end it at that.

"Nh...!!"

The shock of realizing Emi was waiting for him made Maou's body pitch forward, almost losing its footing on the stairs. He had to grab the handrail with both hands to steady himself.

"Ugh, don't fall. I'm not kindhearted enough to catch you if you do."

"E-Emi," Maou stammered at the half-joking voice from below. Then he fell silent. He had her attention, but no idea what to ask. But Emi, understanding what was on his mind, gave him a faint smile.

"What made you want to work at that place anyway, Devil King?"

"...Um?"

Maou didn't understand the point of the sudden question, but it was still far more comprehensible than most of Emi's behavior today. "Well," he meekly explained, "they were okay with zero experience, it was close to this apartment, and I figured I could score some free food out of it. Also, like maybe I told you before, I could get promoted to a permanent position..."

"Right, so you had a lot of motivations to work besides just money. And I'm the same way."

"Oh?"

Emi took her eyes off Maou, directing them toward the Villa Rosa building.

"I had Father and Bell look after Alas Ramus during my interview today. Dokodemo paid well, but I couldn't let her come out in physical form all day, so I felt kind of bad for her. If I worked over there, though, she could stay here and not feel all cooped up inside me. Bell said I probably couldn't take Alas Ramus into the restaurant itself, but..."

She smiled, perhaps recalling the story of the chaos Maou and Chiho inadvertently caused with Alas Ramus at MgRonald.

"So I decided on that once Father was set to move her. That I'd work there for my next job. I was pretty sure they'd hire me—you kept harping at me about how short on people you are, and I figured my phone experience would help out for the big delivery launch."

She exhaled deeply. "So I'm not doing this because you asked me, or because I'm just going with the flow. I applied at the MgRonald by Hatagaya station of my own free will. I wanted to work there because it's the most ideal place for me right now. So that's why I interviewed."

This still left Maou less than satisfied, but he had nothing to counter with.

"I'm glad I stayed here tonight. I got to repay you and fully thank you for Efzahan."

"Emi, you…" Maou looked at Emi's face, lit up by the moon above.

"And starting tomorrow, I'll be moving forward again."

She flashed a pure, guileless smile at him.

"…"

Silent, Maou thought it looked familiar. Where had he seen it before? It was only once, but he was sure he had seen a similarly honest, non-ironic smile from her before. He couldn't remember when.

And that…

"Oh, speaking of which…"

…was because Emi…

"Kisaki remembered who I was, like I figured she would. We got to talking about you and Chiho—it was kind of just chatting, for a lot of it. And if I'm really hired, we're gonna have to conform to company policy when we're around her. So…"

…gave him the shock of his life.

"…it's gonna be first names from now on. Good to work with ya, Sadao!"

"Whoooaaaaaaaa?!"

At that moment, despite standing bolt upright, Maou still slipped on the stairs. He fell forward, annoying the neighbors with his primal scream as he did. All three of the upstairs residents came out the Room 201 door, as did Nord from his own apartment, carrying Alas Ramus.

"My liege! What happened?!"

"Maou?!"

"Not again, Emilia..."

"What is the meaning of this noise?!"

"Mmm...nffhh..."

They were greeted by the sight of Maou sprawled out at the bottom of the stairs, covered in dust, along with Emi, who had to step aside to avoid him.

"Um, are you all right? I said I wouldn't catch you, but the way you fell, I couldn't have done much even if I wanted to."

"Oh. Ah...oh," Maou exercised his lungs enough to groan. His eyes, as he stared at Emi above, housed a palpable sort of terror. "You... You... That..."

"What? You hate it that much?"

Emi must have known. But she played the fool and asked anyway. The evidence for this: the laugh she had just barely avoided bursting out with.

"Well, fine, then. Like I said, I haven't forgiven you. I'm gonna relish calling you that for a while, Sada—"

"Noooooo!!"

Maou shot up to his feet, using all four of his limbs to crawl up the stairs, slink his way between Chiho and Ashiya on the hallway, and plunge into his apartment.

"What has gotten into him?" Suzuno audibly wondered from the side. But once the door was closed, they began to hear sounds from inside. She knocked. "Hey! Devil King! Don't lock the door! What are you doing?!"

"M-Maou! Maou, open up! My stuff is still in your room..."

"What is the meaning of this, my liege? I'm opening the door."

"Keep it *closed*, Ashiyaaaaaa!"

Ignoring the pained scream of the King of All Demons, Ashiya took a key out from his apron pocket and unlocked the door.

"Ah-ha-ha-ha-ha-ha-ha!"

It was too much for Emi to bear. Now her laughter was all too audible.

"Mm?" Nord asked, rubbing his eyes. "Emilia, what happened?"

Emi shook her head, still smiling. "Nothing, nothing. Sorry we were so loud this late." Then she waved at the still-dumbfounded Chiho and Suzuno above and stepped into Room 101. "At least now, though, it's all over."

"Hmm?"

Nord cocked an eyebrow, not understanding what she meant. But Emi couldn't have looked more refreshed.

"Tomorrow," she declared in the moonlight that illuminated their room, "it's gonna be a whole new world. I think I'm gonna sleep like a baby tonight."

Given the continued noise from the chaotic confusion above, Nord wasn't so sure.

THE DEVIL
AND THE
HERO
FULFILL A
DELAYED
PROMISE

There is never any predicting what tomorrow may bring, Ashiya thought, deep inside his mind, as he sized Maou up. It was almost to the point in the morning where he'd be late for work if he didn't leave now, but he absolutely refused to take a step away from the front door.

"Your Demonic Highness," he attempted, "you simply must go to work. Another moment, and you will miss the beginning of your shift."

"…"

The plea did nothing to make Maou move a muscle.

"Acting this way will do nothing to change the facts. I am afraid you must resign yourself to reality."

"…"

"My liege, please, pull yourself together! If this is how you act on the first day, I cannot even fathom what the future holds."

"…Ashiyaaa."

"Yes, my liege?"

"I…" Maou's spine shuddered. "I've never felt this way beforrre…"

"Yes?"

He turned his ashen face toward Ashiya.

"I don't wanna go to worrrk!!"

The next moment, Maou was summarily thrown out of his own apartment.

"I want you to go straight to work, my liege!" Ashiya shouted from the stairway as Maou lazily, wobbily pedaled Dullahan II away from his apartment. He waved a limp arm behind him in response.

This was the kind of demon who often babbled in his sleep about his job. But since last night, it was "I don't wanna go to work" this, "I gotta get outta work" that, "I wanna take off tomorrow" the other thing. It made him sound uncannily like Urushihara. And normally Ashiya would take every measure to care for his superior after such a traumatic experience, but this time—given the circumstances that triggered it—he had little sympathy. He had to put his foot down—his master needed to get out there.

"Is the Devil King gone?"

"Yes," Ashiya listlessly replied to Suzuno, who'd waited until Maou was fully out of sight.

"I heard most of his carrying on, but do you believe he is truly that depressed about his job situation?"

"Ah, I never wanted to see His Demonic Highness in such a state…"

"I imagine not, no. There is not a single person in this world who wants to see the Devil King wheedle his way out of work, as if he were Lucifer or the like."

It was not exactly her problem, but even so, the sympathy was clear in her voice.

"So today is Emilia's first day?"

"That it is, yes," Ashiya sighed. "She volunteered for quite a packed shift schedule, she told me. Attempting to make up for the cut in pay, I would imagine. We are unlikely to see a day when her shift does not overlap with my liege's. Which means…"

"The Devil King is in charge of training her?"

"As likely as not, as he put it. He is the only crewmember besides Ms. Kisaki who is capable of running the upstairs café space solo, so perhaps there is a decent chance that someone running the regular-menu counter will be responsible instead."

Such was Maou's theory last night, one expressed with all the hope and expectation he could muster.

"But why not Chiho, I wonder? She has the experience to train her, no?"

"Ms. Sasaki is a capable worker, but she is still in high school. In fact, she has only been on the staff for half a year, still. A training role for her would still be a tad hasty, although it is Ms. Kisaki's choice in the end."

Three days had passed since Emi's shocker of a job interview at the MgRonald in Hatagaya. Her first stint on the clock would begin this evening. Maou had spent the interval probing for any excuse, any escape valve that would keep him from going to work, all of which had failed due to Ashiya playing interference. Ashiya was not at all interested in seeing Maou flee like a scurrying rat from Emi; in fact, the thought of the Devil King getting to treat the Hero as a lackey, a subordinate fit for nothing but insults and abuse, energized him. But something about the scenario terrorized Maou so much that he refused to listen to any of his Demon General's advice.

It was Maou leaving his phone in Ashiya's possession that doomed him. In the end, their concerns about Urushihara using Maou's credit card without permission proved unfounded. But Maou wanted to call MgRonald to schedule a different shift for himself—a disgraceful act, as far as Ashiya was concerned. So for now, the phone was still with him.

In the end, finally painted into a corner, last night Maou started going on about using his demonic force to change the shift schedule, or faking an illness. That earned him one of the most blistering scoldings Ashiya had dished out in recent memory. The sorry sight of the Devil King wasting his energy on such pathetic measures—it was deplorable.

And it all happened in those few minutes his eyes were off him, those few moments when he chased Emi out of Devil's Castle and took a tumble down the stairs. *Something* happened, Maou refused to say what, and Chiho and Suzuno had no ideas, either. Suzuno seemed to indicate that she had an inkling, but offered little in the way of concrete conclusions to him.

"I do hope this does not affect his work performance," Ashiya gloomily muttered.

"We will have to hope Chiho provides him with ample support. Ah, but if today is Emilia's first day... Alciel, do you have a spare moment today? I would like to discuss something with you and Nord later."

"...Rather sudden. What is it?"

It was rare for Suzuno to ask Ashiya for advice. But she almost seemed to be looking forward to it. "Nothing of great importance," she said. "But if this is Emilia's first day at work, I thought it might be time to act upon our plan, as late as it comes."

"Plan?" Ashiya asked, confused, as Suzuno took out her phone and began to call someone.

"One moment. I'd like to speak to Rika, and Emeralda should still be here as well. I suppose it is best to wait until after school hours to contact Chiho."

Ashiya, oblivious to her intentions, could only stand there and give Suzuno a perplexed look.

✳

To Maou, the MgRonald by Hatagaya station was a place of solace, an oasis of calm in a way that Room 201 at Villa Rosa wasn't. Or at least that's how it had been.

The brisk, controlled chaos inside reminded him of the great fields of battle he had presided over during his world-conquest years. The work gave him courage, helping him keep his mind focused on his foremost goals.

And all it took to change everything was the appearance of a single person. He couldn't relax—it felt like someone's eyes were always on him. Someone calling for him sent a chill up and down his spine, freezing him on the spot. The poison-tipped stares from Kawata, not to mention the rest of the male crewmembers, stabbed into him. His most trusted work friends! And it was all thanks to *her*.

"Hey, Mr. Maou, is this the right way to change out the orange juice concentrate?"

"Y-yeah…"

"Mr. Maou, we're running short on take-out paper bags. Can I go get some more?"

"S-sure…"

"Um, Mr. Maou, these two dust cloths for the seats are pretty worn out. Is it okay to throw them out and bring out some new ones?"

"………………………………………………………………………………
………………………………………………………………'Kay."

Emi was standing next to him, her long hair tied back like Kisaki's, and from day one, she was carrying out her work with the aura of a seasoned veteran. Kisaki knew they were already acquainted, and so of *course* she assigned him to train her—a cruel fate that proved just as unavoidable as he'd feared.

Several crewmembers remembered her as well, Kawata included, and given how Emi generally fell into the "easy on the eyes" category, the cries of protest the other men gave upon hearing that Maou was training her were both impassioned and actually kind of serious. "I hope all that good luck kills you," Kawata told him in the break room. Maou knew he was all but pleading for a wife, but still, that assessment wasn't exactly welcome news for Maou. Kawata had another young woman to train, the second hire from Kisaki's day-long interview session, but—just as he had lamented earlier—this girl was happily married.

But even the Devil King, who yearned for Emi to leave his oasis, had to admit that the Hero was an extremely talented hire. Teach her something once, and she did it perfectly each time after that. From the sample dialogue in the manual to the names and locations of the tray papers, napkins, ketchup, mustard, syrup, and milk, as well as when they needed replenishing, it was all flawless. Given her experience dealing with faceless voices at the call center, she made a clear effort to act more cheerful and energetic around the customers she faced; Kisaki praised her vocal skills practically from day one.

The questions Emi had been lobbing at Maou weren't major ones; they all just came from her lack of experience with MgRonald's standards and unwritten customs. Once she grasped all of them, she wouldn't have to rely on anyone else for her work duties. That was how much her work ethic and memory skills stood out.

"Marko?" Kisaki said, marveling at Emi's effort.

"...Yes?"

"Could you tell Ms. Yusa that I'd like her to try everything on the menu as soon as she can?"

Not even Kisaki was the kind of manager to give Emi her official nickname on the very first day, but she was still impressed enough that she apparently wanted her to master the food offerings in short order.

"...I wish her training period would end already, dang." Maou sighed as he fetched two new dust cloths from the stockroom.

Emi whirled around. She must have felt his gaze on her.

"Hmm? Sorry, was there a problem, Mr. Maou?"

"Huh? Oh, uhh, no, nothing."

"Oh?"

Being called out didn't exactly fill Maou with shame. He had no reason to struggle for a response like that. But in the scant few hours that Emi had been on duty, Maou's spirits were already flagging desperately. Here was this girl who called him everything up to "a blood-sucking monster lowlife cockroach," and now she was using that same mouth to say "Mr. Maou."

It'd be too untoward, Maou claimed, for Emi to casually use Maou's first name quite yet. It'd set a bad example for the rest of the crew. Thus, Maou pleaded with her to at least keep it to that, and not "Sadao" like she had threatened earlier. So "Maou" it was, with the "Mr." part added so she didn't seem too familiar with him in the rest of the staff's eyes. It was strange—Chiho or anyone else calling him that was never a problem, but for some reason, Emi calling him by name made him shudder.

Using the new cloth to wipe up the stack of used trays, Emi picked up the pile and ferried it over to the fresh stack by the counter. As she did, she passed by Maou's side. "Devil King," she whispered.

"Um, what...?"

"I know you're not exactly thrilled to partner with me, but you're really harshing people's buzz around here right now. That's not good for the place, is it?"

"...!!" Hearing the advice, Maou opened his eyes wide...and began to laugh a tense, suppressed laugh. "Heh...heh-heh-heh-heh... Look at you! A total rookie, saying self-important things like that, huh? Well, all right..."

Nearly wild-eyed, he flashed Emi the brightest, most businesslike smile he could muster. "Ms. Yusa."

"Y-yes?" Emi stammered, a little unnerved by his eerie behavior. Something about the tenor of "Ms. Yusa," whenever Maou used it to refer to her at work, seemed tremendously off-putting. They never bothered with formalities like that in real life, so the simple addition of "Ms." was enough to send an indescribable chill down her spine.

"If that's how you're gonna act around here... Ms. Kisaki didn't have any instructions for you, but for as long as time allows, I'm gonna jam you with as much work as I possibly can, got it?"

"Um, sure? The more veteran instruction I can receive, the better."

"You're on, Ms. Yusa!!"

"Bring it, Mr. Maou!!"

"Heh-heh-heh-heh..." they both laughed.

"What is *with* them?" Kawata asked as he passed by, the very air surrounding Maou and Emi seeming to twist and swirl around them in his eyes. He felt obliged to squint for a moment, to make sure he wasn't imagining it.

"Right! You're gonna get no mercy, you got that? Let's start with using the soft-cream machine to make the dessert menu! You'll be the new girl *forever* if you can't do that!"

"Ha! Give me everything you've got! I'll make it all!"

"I'm only gonna teach you once, so listen up! Before you touch the bar on the machine, always spray your hands with that disinfectant! Down to the *wrists*, you hear me?"

"You don't need to tell *me* twice!!"

"Listen up! We'll start with a cone! That's part of the hundred-yen menu! You let the cream fall straight into the cone! When it reaches the upper lip, you spin the cone around for *exactly* two-and-a-half revolutions! You hearing me? There's kind of a trick to crafting the little 'swirly' on the top! If you can't pull that off, you aren't worthy to even lick my boots!"

"Pfft! I used to work in a *real* office, you know! A lot of quick-service joints have you operate the ice-cream machine by yourself these days, too! If you think I'm a total newbie to this, you're gonna pay dearly for it!"

"Hah! Don't make me laugh! If you think the soft cream at the Mag is the same as that crap from the self-serve joints, you got another think coming! MgRonald's ice cream is made with milk sourced one hundred percent from dairy farms in Hokkaido! It's smooth, creamy, and heavier than most ice cream, so it ain't gonna be that easy to stack those two-and-a-half twirls, girl!"

"What is with them, seriously?" Kawata shrugged as he left the scene, unsure if this was a training seminar or a lovers' spat.

But unlike him, there was someone else watching who knew exactly what fueled this tension. It was Chiho, of course, peering at them intently from outside the glass door out front. "...Well, good," she said. "Glad it's going all right, more or less."

Once, not that long ago, it was Emi watching Maou and Chiho from her hiding place outside MgRonald. Now the tables were turned. She was coming home from school when she began worrying about them openly quarreling at work, so she stopped over to check despite not having a shift, just to make sure.

Even from outside the dining-room space, she could tell that the tension inside was going in kind of an odd direction. But they weren't coming to blows, at least, which came as a huge relief.

She realized she was a bit hungry, even though dinner was coming

up. *I'm here and all,* she thought. *Maybe I ought to stop in as a customer while I'm at it, too.*

Before she could act on the impulse, the phone in her school-uniform jacket rang. She locked at the screen.

"Huh? Maou?"

It was from the number that belonged to Maou, who was clearly busy haranguing Emi at the moment. She answered it.

"Hello, is this Ms. Sasaki? It is I, Ashiya."

"Oh, Ashiya! I was wondering why Maou would be calling me in the middle of his work shift."

"Ah, indeed. I had to borrow the Devil King's cell phone for...reasons, earlier. Are you home from school?"

"Oh, um, I'm actually in front of MgRonald because I was worried about how Maou and Emi were doing, but it seems from here that it's not going so bad."

"Yes? Well, quite good, then. In that case, I apologize for asking this so abruptly..."

"Yes?"

"Do you know if Ms. Kisaki is at the restaurant today?"

"Um, Ms. Kisaki?" Chiho repeated, surprised at the question.

"Indeed. Because if she is, there is a favor I would like to ask of her. I could always try another day if not, however..."

"Well, wait just one sec. I'll check the shift schedule real quick." Chiho took a notebook out of her bag and extracted the schedule she always had tucked inside it.

"Umm... Oh, Kisaki's got last shift today. She'll be there for closing with Maou. Emi's still in training, so she'll probably get off around ten... Ooh, I didn't realize it was just Maou and Kisaki from ten 'til closing. Maybe they'll close the café counter early, then. When it's slow at night, sometimes they keep the upstairs unmanned unless a customer requests it."

"I see. One moment, then... Bell, Ms. Sasaki says Ms. Kisaki is on duty."

Chiho could hear Ashiya exchange a few words with Suzuno,

presumably in the room with him, along with someone else she couldn't quite identify.

"*Right, my apologies about this, Ms. Sasaki.*"

"No prob."

"*So if Bell came to pick up you around ten tonight, do you think you'd be able to go out with her?*"

"Huh?" Chiho blinked.

"God...damn it..."

Maou, drained by waves of fatigue, was on his knees.

"Hmph."

Emi, meanwhile, puffed her chest out in supreme triumph, staring coldly downward at him.

It was ten PM at the first-floor counter, with Emi almost free of duty, and she was just about to conduct a postmortem review of her training with Maou and Kisaki.

"So how was your first day?" a smiling Kisaki asked Emi, even as she noticed Maou's pathetic act off to the side.

"Quite fulfilling, thanks. Mr. Maou sure taught me a lot."

"Ngh..."

Maou had no words to counter with.

Emi had conquered the soft-cream machine. Mastering every item on the dessert menu that relied on ice cream in a single day was abnormal in itself. It wasn't a machine they were even supposed to cover on the first day. But she tackled it anyway, taking notes when needed and grasping Maou's instructions almost perfectly. She even successfully took the machine apart for cleaning, with nothing but verbal instructions to rely on.

"It's still my first day, though," she continued, "and there's a lot to the menu I'm not fully versed in yet. I think I'll have a lot to learn from Mr. Maou tomorrow, too."

"Mm-hmm. And how was it for you, Marko?"

"Um..." He looked up blankly, eyes turning to Emi's face for just a single instant. "I mean, frankly... She was perfect. She's such a quick learner, and with her experience in phone service, she seemed to get along really well with the customers."

"True. That was my impression, too. You're already an expert, kind of."

Emi nodded her appreciation. "Thank you very much! I'm glad to hear that."

"If you ask me, I think she'll be ready to handle the register before too long."

It was half flattery, half the honest truth from Maou, who hoped to escape the training gauntlet with her as soon as he could.

"Mmm," Kisaki replied. "Well, no need to go diving in the deep end, either. I hope you'll be working just as hard going forward as you did today...or harder, even. Not to gush too much in front of Marko, but you might just surpass his feat of legend someday."

"Oh, man..." Maou brought a hand to his head, unexpectedly pierced to the core by this unexpected arrow from his manager. She was playing him like a fiddle, and he knew it.

The "feat of legend" she referred to was the way Maou got a 100-yen-an-hour pay raise a mere month after wrapping up his training. Having Emi beat that would be more than regrettable to him— it'd be a tragedy. As a MgRonald crewmember, and as Devil King.

"Well," Kisaki said, "glad to hear there weren't any major hitches. Good work."

"Thank you very much," Emi said, smiling as she bowed a bit and made for the break room.

"Oh, by the way," Kisaki called at her from behind. "I apologize, Ms. Yusa, but could I speak to you for a moment when you're done changing?"

"Sure. What about?"

"Well, go get changed first. We can talk after that. I have a quick phone call to make, Marko."

"Oh...?"

Maou and Emi exchanged looks with each other before Emi headed toward the staff room again. Kisaki, meanwhile, punched a number into the restaurant phone's receiver.

"Hello? Chi? It's Kisaki. You free right now? Okay. I think we'll be able to pull this off... Ten minutes? Got it. I'll be here."

"...You were calling Chi? What's happening in ten minutes?"

"Oh, well, you'll see. I know I don't say this too often, but let's just hope we don't get an onrush of customers for a little while."

"All...right...?"

The uncharacteristic statement gave Maou pause. Just long enough of a pause, it turned out, to let Emi return from the break room in her own clothing.

Kisaki looked at her watch and nodded. "Right on time."

"What is?" Emi asked.

Their manager simply motioned toward the front entrance. Maou and Emi followed her gaze.

"...Huh?"

"Uhh?"

They were both awed by the group that suddenly walked through the automatic door. Chiho was in the lead, followed by Ashiya, Suzuno, Nord, Alas Ramus, Acieth, Emeralda, and Rika—the whole gang.

"Good evening, Yusa! Hi, Maou!"

"Pardon us, if you would."

"Excuse our rudeness."

"Hello..."

"Magrobbld!"

"Hi-hiiiii!"

"Keep up the good worrrk, guys."

"Yo! Emi! You made it!"

All the greetings and praise thrown toward them in unison threw Emi and Maou for a loop. They were even more surprised to see Kisaki walk up to Chiho, like nothing was abnormal about this, and point upstairs.

"Well, lucky for you but not so lucky for us, there's nobody on the second floor. I can't have you hang around for too long, but feel free to take the two tables on the far end."

"Sure thing! Thanks for being such a good sport about this!"

"Hey, you can just pay me back with your next shift, huh?" Kisaki adjusted her visor and turned to Maou and Emi. "...You two head on up too, all right? I can't run the whole place by myself for too long. Take 'em to the tables on the far side. I'll run things down here for the time being."

"Huh? Really? Eme, and Father, and Rika, even? Why are you...?"

"Take them...? Ms. Kisaki, what's going on here...?"

"Come on, Maou, before anyone else shows up!"

"You too, Emi! We can't waste a bunch of your manager's time."

Chiho grabbed the still-dumbfounded Maou's arm, Rika doing the same with Emi, as they dragged them upstairs and to the two windowside tables at the otherwise-empty café space.

"All right, Emi, you sit next to Chiho."

The two of them were the first to sit. They were both presented with a large, gift-wrapped box—and upon closer inspection, they realized the wrapping had a MgRonald-logo pattern on it.

Maou spotted it right off. "Wait," he yelped, "is this...? You guys actually roped Kisaki into doing it here...?"

"Hey, it's official MgRonald stuff, okay?" Rika explained. "That's why the manager said yes to it. C'mon, we can't waste any time! Ashiya, open it up!"

"As you wish."

He neatly, nimbly undid the wrapping. Inside was a white cardboard box, a slightly sweet scent wafting out from it. Emi, still a little bewildered, watched as Rika grabbed it from the side.

"Okay, you guys..."

"Huh? Huh?"

"Let's do it!" Chiho gleefully shouted.

With an equally cheerful squeal, Rika opened it up.

"Happy birthday, guys!!"

"...!!!!" Emi gasped, covering her mouth with both hands.

From out of the box, a simple-looking shortcake appeared. What separated it from the usual grocery-store fare was the disc of white chocolate that topped it, the MgRonald logo and the words "Happy Birthday!" engraved upon it

"Chiho, this, this…"

Emi's voice was already as wavering as her own psyche at this point.

"I know our plans kind of went awry," Chiho said, "and it's not exactly anyone's birthday any longer…" She paused, hesitant, then nodded. "But today's the start of a new journey for you, Yusa, so we all figured, if not now, when?"

"G-guys…"

Emi looked around her, not bothering to hide the moisture gathering in her eyes.

"I mean, *whew*, when Suzuno called to invite me to this, I was all like, 'Sure, let's do it!' But, like, that was earlier today! Kind of short notice to find a cake like this!"

"W-wait," Maou interjected. "Aren't these only available at Mg-Ronald locations that actually offer birthday parties? Don't you have to reserve these way in advance?!"

"Indeed," Ashiya confirmed. "This is not, strictly speaking, an official MgRonald product. We had a local bakery modify a generic cake for us, and your manager was nice enough to bend the rules a little."

"That… You guys…"

"She agreed to it as long as the cake was branded with the MgRonald logo…and as long as we did something else."

"Wh-what?"

"She said we could borrow this space for half an hour," Rika interjected again, "as long as each of us ordered a combo meal worth six hundred yen or more."

"Oh," Maou said, still bewildered, as he recalled his training. "Right, everyone at an official birthday party needs to buy a combo, right…?"

"That," said Suzuno, "and after checking about the differences in calendars between our worlds with Emeralda, we've learned that Emilia's birthday on Ente Isla occurs one week from today. October the twenty-fifth in this world."

"It…does, Bell?"

"Yeah! And…" Rika lowered her voice a little, ensuring Kisaki couldn't hear her downstairs. "I asked Emeralda, and she said you're actually turning eighteen this year? 'Cause, *boy*, what a surprise! You're so mature, I never woulda guessed you're younger than me. But I'll whack you one if you start actin' all polite around me, okay?"

"Rika… Um, thanks. Thank you…!" Tears were already starting to free themselves from Emi's eyes. "Chiho… I…!"

"Yusa?"

Emi hugged the teenage girl next to her, not bothering to wipe the tears from her face. Chiho returned the gesture. "Welcome back home," she whispered into her ear. "And happy birthday, too."

"Th… Thanks…! You too, Chiho!"

She quietly shed her tears, Chiho's following soon behind. Nord, looking on, felt his own emotions stir as well.

"You have been blessed…with good friends, Emilia."

"She certainly has," Emeralda affectionately added.

"Right! We don't have much time, so let's keep it going! Time to give out the presents before the customers downstairs see us!"

"Oh, um, s-sure, but I, I didn't get anything for…"

"Of course you didn't get anything for Chiho, Emi! This was a surprise! You can worry about that later, okay? Let's start with the rest of the gang. Suzuno?"

"Yes. We all selected this today—Nord, Emeralda, Alciel, and myself."

"Huh? Ashiya, what are you—*ow*!"

"Quit complaaaining," Emeralda warned, fresh from kicking Maou in the shin, "or else I'll wad you up and throw you in the garrrbage."

"Well, thank you. I wonder what it is… Wait." Wiping her tears, Emi looked up at Suzuno, a look of realization dawning on her face. "Bell, what are you wearing?"

"Oh, erm…"

"Yeah, cute, huh? Me and Chiho chose it for her."

"I-I feel it does not look too strange on me, but what do you think?"

Suzuno, Emi's present in her arms, was not in her usual Japanese-style dress. Instead, she sported a navy-blue flared skirt, a pair of camel boots, and a navy striped blouse topped with a broad-collared, cream-white sweater. All Western wear.

"Oh, it's not strange at all! It's really cute!"

"Is… Is it? They told me we would stand out too much if I wore a kimono during this party, so…" She mumbled the words, her face a bit red. "Um, I decided to try this out for the first time… I find this frilly skirt may take some getting used to, but as long as it looks natural, very well… But, but enough of me!" she said, thrusting the box in her hands toward Emi and Chiho. "Here!"

"Thanks. It really does look good on you."

"Enough of that!"

Emi smiled at the unusually bashful Suzuno and opened the box.

"Ooh, it's a photo frame! I like the design on it!"

In the box was a glass photo frame, blue with a few seagulls around it. It was a joy for Emi to discover.

"We were unsure what to buy, but it was Alciel's ingenious idea."

"Alciel?"

"I told you it was better left unsaid," Ashiya sulked, before realizing that Emi was looking right at him curiously. "…But you are with your father again," he bluntly stated. "You will be making more memories with him, and I thought you might want something to display them with. That was all I said."

"Oh… Yeah. You're right," Emi said as she clutched the frame to her chest.

"We have a matching one for you as well, Chiho. I hope you will enjoy it."

"Wow! A matching one?!"

Chiho removed the wrapping from her own box, revealing a glass photo frame like Emi's, except done up in pink.

"Ooh, it really does match!" Emi observed.

"This is so great! Thanks! I feel kind of bad now, though…"

"Oh?"

"I mean, I gotta hand it to Ashiya, I guess…or I guess we were both thinking the same thing." Bashfully, Chiho presented Emi with her own wrapped package. "I, um, kinda got you a picture frame, too."

Her box was a level larger than the one Suzuno had brought. Emi opened it, revealing a metallic frame decorated with enamel and gem-like designs, with a few different compartments for displaying multiple photos.

"I want you to have a lot of memories around," Chiho explained, "so I chose that one. I feel bad that it's the same as Ashiya's idea, but..."

"Oh, Chiho... That's really sweet, though, that you thought of that by yourself. Thank you so much. I'll keep this someplace special."

She placed Chiho's frame on the table and hugged her once more.

Next came the night's star performer.

"Hee-hee-heeeeee! I was actually thinking about a photo frame, too. Good thing I didn't go through with it!"

Rika took out a box, this one notably thicker than the ones before.

"But when I thought about where'd we be, this popped right into my mind! Check it out, Emi! Here's what I really feel about you!"

"Thanks. Can I open it?"

She accepted the slightly heavy package and opened the lid. Inside was what at first appeared to be a wooden box, with a brass windup knob on one side and a musical note engraved on the lid.

"It's a music box?"

"Sure is! Open it, open it!"

Popping it open, Emi found a glass sheet covering the inner side of the lid.

"You can stick a photograph in that panel," Rika said, leaning back in her chair.

There was a pause. Then:

"Uh, so it's still a photo frame?"

It was Maou who dared bring it up first.

"Aw, c'mon! Like, if you think about where Emi is in her life, like, what *else* is gonna come to mind?" Rika smiled and tapped her head with a finger. "And thanks for the zinger, Maou. It's still *mostly* a music box, all right? And check out the title."

She pointed at an engraving on the side of box. HAPPY BIRTHDAY TO YOU, it read.

"Rika, is that...?"

"We'd probably get yelled at if we all sang it in here, but I thought it'd be nice if we could still express that in music. Play it once you get back home."

Emi found herself having to resist the urge to wind it up and listen to it right there—this piece of music so intertwined with Rika's own feelings for her.

"And I got this for Chiho. You won't see a gift like this from any-one except for me, I guarantee it!"

"Oh, you have one for me, too?"

Chiho's eyes goggled. She must not have expected anything from Rika.

"Suzuno told me this would be a tandem party for you two, so... Open it up!"

"O-okay. Thank you... Ah!"

The box she handed her contained a small perfume bottle. It was engraved with the logo of a famous cosmetic brand, and the name of the scent was, following the night's theme, "Happy Birthday."

"I dunno if you'll like the scent or not," Rika explained, sidling up to Chiho's side, "but you can just treat it as a message of support from me, y'know?"

"Umm..." a flustered Chiho began.

"You're gonna need at least one adult fragrance for your future. Take that perfume and polish up your womanly wiles for the guy of your dreams!"

"M-Ms. Suzuki!!"

Chiho fell into a panic, realizing that Rika's eyes were tilted ever-so-slightly toward Maou.

"Ooh, Grampa, Grampa! That thing!"

"Oh, er, yes. Alas Ramus insisted, you see..."

Now it was Nord and Alas Ramus's turn.

"Mommy, Chi-sis, happy birfday!"

With the well-wishes came a slightly warped piece of drawing paper from Nord. Sizing it up, Emi and Chiho immediately flashed bright smiles. It was a portrait of the two of them, rendered lovingly by Alas Ramus using a wide variety of crayon colors. The two of them stood next to each other, standing atop a field of green in front of some kind of large, brown box—Villa Rosa Sasazuka, no doubt. It was clearly a labor of love, just the sort of thing Alas Ramus loved doing, and it was charming enough to steal the heart of any grown-up in attendance.

"I suppose she's a born artist," Nord said with a laugh. "She drew the same piece several times before she had one she was satisfied with."

"Ooh, I want all of 'em."

"Me too. Otherwise, Chiho and I are probably gonna fight over this one."

Emi took another loving look at the work of art.

"Guys… Thank you all so much. I'm never gonna forget this day, seriously…"

"Ohhh, hang on," interrupted Rika. "Save your thanks for later, Emi. I think someone else still needs to speak up?"

Emi fell silent, surprised. A little ways from the table, Maou awkwardly stood, his ribs currently getting elbowed by Acieth. "Come on, Maou," she pleaded. "The thing you chose, before, why not give now?"

"…Uh-uh. I didn't know this was gonna happen. I don't even have it on—"

"Is this what you are looking for?" Suzuno said, stopping him cold as she produced three small, oblong, gift-wrapped boxes. It instantly made Maou's face tense.

"Whoa, did, did you…?"

"Acieth told me you had purchased something for Chiho and Emilia, Devil King. So I asked Alciel about it. He found these in your modular shelving."

"Gehh!"

"She said you purchased these as souvenirs after Albert and I left you? To make up for matters?"

"Aciethhhh?!"

"Oh, come on, Maouuuu!" she shouted as Maou roughly shook her by the shoulders. "You say it yourself, there!"

It took Suzuno to pull him away from her—by the head—and march him back in front of Emi and Chiho. She shoved the three boxes in his face, a look of supreme satisfaction on her own. "I appreciate the spirit behind the purchase," she whispered to him, "and thus I will overlook the way you used my money for it."

"Ngh..."

Maou accepted the boxes, and the intention behind her veiled threat.

"But where did you get these boxed? They were loose when I got home, after we fell in that pond..."

"Alciel is a skillful demon," Suzuno replied. "I gave him some cardboard and wrapping paper, and he made these for you."

Maou glared at Ashiya. Ashiya took the opportunity to stare into space.

The boxes, of course, contained a set of three carved wooden spoons, purchased in the outskirts of Heavensky with money borrowed from Suzuno. He had purchased a flower-pattern one for Chiho and a pair decorated with birds for Emi and Alas Ramus, but standing here and being asked to give the last present of the evening made it incredibly awkward for him. He had never imagined in a million years that Suzuno and his other acquaintances would organize such a dramatic event. Compared to the other presents, it felt like there was no real thought, or heartful emotion, to his.

"...So, um..."

But it was too late to excuse himself. Maou braced himself and presented the boxes to the two birthday girls.

"I bought these just in case we ever did this, so... Hope you can use 'em. I got two for you, Emi, so Alas Ramus can have one. I think they're supposed to bring good luck or something?"

As a speech, it lacked much in the way of a coherent theme. Emi and Chiho accepted the bluntly offered gifts regardless.

"Can I open this?"

"…Uh, yeah? It's a present," came the blunt reply. They obeyed him.

"…Ah…"

Then, seeing the contents, they both gasped in unison. Rika and Emeralda curiously leaned in from the side.

"What's that? …Ooh, that's nice!"

"What waaas it? …Ahh. Very cuuute."

The onlookers sounded far more enthusiastic about the gifts, these spoons carved from a single piece of wood, than the actual recipients. Chiho was still silent, scrutinizing the pattern on hers—a flower in bloom, with five broad petals—until she sighed. "What a mysterious design… It's so beautiful."

"I've never seen anything like this," Emi said, comparing the small differences between the bird patterns in her two spoons. "I don't see any joints or anything. This was carved straight from one piece, wasn't it? Did you find this in Efzahan?"

"Um, yeah… I figured, you know, they'd be useful, so…"

"They're so pretty," Chiho said, "I'd almost feel bad actually using them. Thank you so much, Maou. I'll take good care of this one, though I might put it on the wall in my room instead."

"Sure, um, I'm glad you like it."

She flashed him a beaming smile, making him nod and nervously bring a hand to his visor.

"She's right," Emi added, a tad emotional as she took up the two spoons. "I'd prefer to have these on display, too. Thank you. I appreciate it."

"…Yeah," Maou just managed to coax out from his throat. He could feel the stares from Chiho, Suzuno, and Ashiya—each with their own feelings about his reaction, no doubt.

"Well," Rika said as she checked her watch, "I hate to rain on the parade, but we better wrap this up. We're already five minutes over, so we ought to clean up and order our meals before the manager gets all snippy. We can do the whole cake-and-candles thing at home, but for dinner, it's gonna be Maggie's or nothing, guys! Oh, and have fun with the rest of your shift, Maou!"

"Yeah, uh, don't wait up for me."

For once, Maou appreciated Rika butting her nose in on matters. If Emi gave him any more of that heartfelt emotion, he wouldn't have been able to take it.

By the time they had the cake back in the box, figured out exactly how Emi and Chiho would carry their presents home, ordered their combo meals and left, it was already past eleven. Maou was the only crewmember on front-end duty, Kisaki handling closing procedures.

"Um, thanks for being so generous with 'em," he said, softly.

"Mm," Kisaki nodded, not bothering to turn around. "Well, anything to boost our sales during dead times like these. It helped both of us out. It's not like they were eating outside food or anything."

"True, but…"

"Oh, but there *is* something I should say."

"Yes?"

Kisaki, despite her disaffectation for the party, turned around to face Maou.

"I'm glad you have such a wide variety of friends of the opposite sex…"

"Yes?"

She sharpened her eyes, almost glaring at Maou.

"But don't do anything that'll make Chi or Ms. Yusa stab you in the back, all right? Because you're way too rough on the women around you…or should I say, it's like you think you can get away with anything around them…"

"Huh?!"

"That's all. Back to work."

"No, wait, um, Ms. Kisaki? I think there might be a pretty big misunderstanding here, but it's really not like that, I promise!"

"Enough. Looking at you, I'm starting to think Kawatchi has a point."

"What'd he say?!"

"Ask him if you want. Something tells me you're gonna be in the doghouse with the male crewmembers for a while."

"Oh, come onnnn!"

"Hey, you reap what you sow."

"I didn't sow anything!!"

The devil's scream roared from the Hatagaya MgRonald, lit by a dazzling full moon, before echoing into the city nightscape.

He was a spent man as he pedaled Dullahan II across the Sasa-zuka neighborhood.

"I've never had…a more tiring shift…"

Simply being Emi's trainer was enough of an emotional strain. Then it was capped off by that surprise birthday party. Sure, they had talked about a party for Chiho and Emi long ago, and Maou had certainly wanted to celebrate Chiho's birthday and make Emi seethe over how much she owed him for the thought. But all that had assumed Maou would play an active part, not simply be a passive participant like this. It was extremely painful to deal with.

And what's more, it ended with:

Thank you. I appreciate it.

Before now, it would have been perfectly in-character for Emi to crush any gift from Maou in a clasped fist, smashing it to atoms.

"What is she even trying to do?!"

She swore she hadn't forgiven him, but now she was obviously opening her heart to him. More than ever before. And Maou wasn't sure how to approach that. Before now, he figured he could just handle her like always. But now, his thoughts turned elsewhere.

"What does 'like always' even *mean*?"

Looking back, Maou had never actively encouraged Emi to do much of anything. Emi kept entangling herself in his life—"you're my enemy" this, "I have to monitor you" that—but Maou had never bothered trying to kick her out, or even figure out what she was doing. In fact, he didn't even know where she lived. He knew it was an apartment in Eifukucho, but he didn't know the address, and he never entertained the idea of finding out.

He kept telling Emi to "go away" whenever she came to his

apartment or workplace, but now it seemed like he accepted her presence in his life all too easily. She wasn't any foe he could defeat in a clash of force, and besides, she never even posed any real threat to his life. And ever since Alas Ramus came along and deepened the links between them in their daily lives, Emi's presence began to seem all the more natural.

So for Maou and Emi's relationship, what "like always" really meant was Maou accepting everything Emi said and did.

"What is the deal with me? I gotta chill out."

"Why are you whining, there?"

Maou was on the side of the road when he heard the voice from above.

"...And what are *you* doing? That's kind of dangerous," he sniffed as he looked up. In the midst of all his musing, he must have finally reached his apartment.

"No, not dangerous. Who you think I am? I could land on head, no injury."

There, on the roof of Villa Rosa Sasazuka, Acieth waved at Maou as she took in the night sky, the nearby light pollution making only the brightest of stars visible.

"I don't care if you're a demon or the Hero. If someone's up there, you warn them. That's it." Maou shrugged and looked at the building. "Wait, where's Emi...?"

"All went home. Chiho has school; Rika has work. Emi took my sister home, too."

That was a relief to Maou. He checked his watch—it was near one in the morning. Not even Chiho could get away with staying at Suzuno's apartment on consecutive days.

"So, what do you mutter and groan about?"

"Shhh. Keep it down."

Acieth was shouting a little, from her perch up on the roof. Maou worried about her waking Suzuno and Nord, not to mention the rest of the neighborhood.

"No. You just come up here. Hup!"

"Huh? Wh-whoa!"

The next moment, before he could even lower the kickstand on Dullahan II, Maou was being lifted into the air.

"Over here. Hup!"

Acieth expertly manipulated Maou in the air, not letting him resist for a moment as she plunked him down next to her, atop the rugged tiles.

"Y-you scared me there..."

"You are Devil King. Flying this much, it should not scare you."

"Anyone would be scared, getting dragged around like that!"

He knew it wasn't the kind of protest Acieth would bother acknowledging.

"So, what do you groan about? Talk to me about anything."

"I'm not desperate enough to ask you of all people for advice."

"Mm? Are you making the fun of me?"

"You know what I mean. So butt out. Sometimes, a man just wants to ponder over stuff by himself."

"Oh, how does saying go...? 'Lame minds think alike'?"

"Wow, way to change a single word to make it sting for me, huh?" Maou sighed and reclined backward. Or tried to. The unbending tiles on the steeply sloped roof convinced him otherwise. "It's kind of...a social issue I'm grappling with."

"Mm? What? Finally decided you will marry Chiho?"

Maou almost fell off the roof entirely. "Who's been blowing *that* into your mind?!!"

"Oh, when we ate, Rika said you were cruel, cruel man, so..."

"Dude, you gotta take whatever that gossip tells you with a grain of salt, all right?!"

"A grain? So, not marry, but she will be concubine to you, or—*ow!*"

"That's not what I meant, and you know it. Where'd you even learn that word, anyway? That's not funny!"

"But that not mean you can punch me!" protested Acieth, rubbing the back of her head as Maou gritted his teeth at her.

"I'm not talking to you about it, all right? If I do, you're gonna twist the story around so much, people are gonna think the sun's rising from the west starting tomorrow."

"Ohhh, I'm sorry. I can listen seriously, okaaaay?"

"Your attitude isn't exactly convincing me, y'know! And what about you? What're you doing up here, late at night?"

"Huh? Oh, yes, the moon is bright tonight, so I look at the sky."

"The sky?"

"Yes. I like looking at the sky in night. But Mikitty's house, the roof is hard to sit on. So, me, I pick here tonight."

"Oh. Great. Just please don't fly over to anybody else's roof, all right?"

Maou winced at all the emergency calls Acieth would generate, wandering from rooftop to rooftop.

"Ooh, I won't! I am not stupid."

That was news to Maou, but following up on it would just rile her up more, so he filed it away in his mind.

"Maou, you were thinking the... Something very rude. Yes?"

"Man, you've got the instincts of a wild animal. But what about you?"

"What?"

"Why'd you pull me up here, anyway? You got something to talk about?"

"Mmm... Talk, maybe, or I think I should tell you?"

"Tell me?"

"Yeah." Acieth lowered her eyebrows a bit as she looked at the moon. "Gabriel, he woke up Our 'discussion' tomorrow, I don't think he can come, but..."

"...Huh." Maou casually nodded at her. "So he's still alive?"

"Ooh? Just...it normal thing to you?"

"Well, 'normal,' I mean... I don't have much of any other reaction."

Gabriel, guardian of the Yesod Sephirah that birthed Alas Ramus and Acieth, had been taken to Japan under Shiba's orders. By the end of the battle in Efzahan and everything else that transpired, he had to be carried over unconscious—a state he had remained in for much longer than Nord, apparently. Maou couldn't say for sure, since unlike Nord, he had holed up inside Shiba's house the entire time; nobody in the apartment building had ever seen him. The demons had no idea how he was doing, and they didn't particularly care to know. They just figured Shiba didn't want to leave him for dead, and considering she had more power than even Maou and Emi could fathom, placing him under her care was about the safest solution they could think of for them all.

"I wish I can send him six feet under again, one more time!"

"Um, you'd have to do it for the first time before that, if you don't mind my saying."

As always, Acieth was oddly hostile toward the angels. Maou was impressed Shiba could wrangle both her and Gabriel under the same roof.

"Yeah," she said, "Mikitty stopped me. Many times."

"She had to do something to stop you?"

"You see! What he did to us. We..." Acieth scowled, then balled herself up a little on the roof. "Not just me and my sister. Erone, and Malkuth, and...everyone..."

"Acieth...?"

"Maou."

"Hmm?"

"What you worry about, I do not know. But talk about it, while we can, still."

"Mm..."

"Or else, maybe we go away from each other, like me and my sister. For ever, and ever, and *evvvvvver*. So, while we can, still."

"...Yeah."

Tomorrow was the day Shiba would gather them all together and give them the whole truth. He had no idea why she wanted to do this around Urushihara's hospital bed, but he assumed they'd know soon enough. And there was that other thought rolling around in his head—the thought that he'd have to reveal some of his own secrets.

"You've...been getting to talk with Alas Ramus?"

"…Yeah. Just chat. In Pop's room."

"Oh."

Now Maou was gently patting Acieth, in the spot where he'd socked her before.

"You know, if you've been separated for that long, I'm sure you've got a lot more to talk about than what you could cover in a week. So take your time with her, okay? Next time something happens to you guys, me and Emi'll step up to protect you."

"Mm…"

Acieth allowed this round of head-patting, but her eyes were sad as she turned toward him.

"Before…"

"Hm?"

"Before, I think…somebody say same thing as you, Maou."

"The same thing?"

"Yeah. It is very long time before, so I do not remember."

Acieth slowly pushed Maou's hand away, stood up, and gently floated down to the apartment's front yard.

"I am glad that we speak. See you tomorrow."

"Uh, sure… Whoa! Wait a sec, Acieth!"

As the girl waved softly at him and walked back to Shiba's house, Maou fell into a sudden panic. Acieth paid it no attention as she walked off. Perhaps he was too far up to be heard.

"Um, how am I supposed to get down…?"

His demonic power was in a nice, neat cube in his closet, but activating it out of the blue might affect Suzuno and Nord in unpredictable ways. Even if it didn't, the sheer force of it could wake them up, and he'd hear no end of it in the morning.

"Geez, I hope I can do this…"

Gingerly, he leaned over the edge of the roof, checking the range between him and the worryingly narrow landing in front of the stairway below. Ever so softly, he lowered himself down, attempting to land in the hallway corridor feet first.

"What are you doing, my liege?"

"Whoahh!!"

Instead, a sudden query from below startled him. His foot slipped, and he just barely managed to grab on to the roof's edge.

"You were awake, Ashiya? Don't scare me like that!"

He looked to his side to find a sleepy-eyed Ashiya poking his head out the Room 201 window.

"You are the one scaring me, if anything. I was wondering what that creaking from the roof was... I never expected Your Demonic Highness would do something as sentimental as climb up to look at the night sky, you see."

"That's seriously not what this is, but could you lend me a hand, already?!"

"Let go, my liege."

"Huhh?!"

"You are just a few inches above the stairs."

"I-I am? You're not lying to me? Well, here I go. If I hurt myself, it's your fault, all right?"

"...Yes, my liege."

"Oof... Oh! Wow, you scared me."

The feeling of terra firma made Maou breathe a sigh of relief. To Ashiya, however, the sight of his master and leader acting too nervous to make a drop of three or four inches without his encouragement made him sigh for different reasons.

"What is the meaning of this? Has working with Emilia driven you to such deep depths of depression?"

"Well, yeah! I *am* depressed! Like never before! I've never been at such an impasse, like... I don't know what to do!"

"Ah..."

"I mean, if we're gonna do it like this, *you* go apply to MgRonald, too! And we'll get Suzuno and Nord and Acieth in there, and then it'll be staffed by nothin' but Ente Islans! Kisaki's gonna be the next queen of our world!"

"There is no need for such despair, my liege. What troubles you, exactly?"

"Nothing! I'm just tired! And hungry! Feed me!"

Maou made for the doorway, storming his way down the corridor.

"Your Demonic Highness, please pick your bicycle up off the ground first."

Ashiya's finger was pointed at Dullahan II, lying on the ground right where Acieth made Maou abandon it. He scowled as he went back downstairs.

"I will heat up a teriyaki burger and some fries for you. We can discuss matters later."

"You bought a combo for *me*, too?! Don't heat up the burger! It'll make the lettuce all limp! I am the Devil King! Why does the Devil King have to hem and haw over stupid crap like this? Damn it!"

Despite all his whining, Maou still carefully parked his bicycle upright before climbing the stairs.

It figured—the night before their big "discussion," and Maou was likely to be ranting well into the night. Ashiya sighed.

✳

Inside his white-walled hospital room, where the color of the sun and the ambient temperature suggested autumn's arrival, Hanzou Urushihara was in his element, his face bathed in the pale blue light from his computer display—until he grimaced in pain.

He recalled the evening that Maou, Suzuno, and Acieth traveled to Ente Isla from the National Museum of Western Art. He had noticed that Chiho was attempting to probe some of Earth and Ente Isla's mysteries with Amane Ohguro, niece of their landlord Miki Shiba and proprietor of the Ohguro-ya snack shop on the Choshi beach. The snippets he could pick up at the time indicated that Chiho wanted him to eavesdrop from Room 201, so he'd thought he'd lend a hand for a change—and *this* was what he'd gotten for it.

A shock like nothing he ever felt before had coursed across his body—not once, but twice. He remembered his state of semiconsciousness, someone barging into his room soon afterward. He still had the wits, apparently, to ask this figure to take his PC along with him. Perhaps he was instinctually bonded to the thing by now.

"So what's the big problem? This oughta be the ideal environment for someone like you, Urushihara."

"And how is *that*?" the fallen angel lashed out at Amane Ohguro, seated in a chair by his bed and watching a travel program she'd picked on the room's TV.

"Well, how do you think? It's your own room. Nobody to bother you. No Maou and Ashiya telling you to get a job. Your meals are all taken care of. For an unemployed bum like you, what more could you ask for?"

"Um, I've got *you* bothering me on a daily basis, the food's all bland and boring, and the Net reception from here sucks, man! Also, I know you ain't the only one, but you got the wrong idea about my Professional Bum lifestyle, too."

"Wrong how?" Amane asked, propping her chair back on two legs like a child as her eyes stayed on the TV. "You looking for some more luxury?"

"No. The thing about bums like me, or your garden-variety shut-ins, is that they always have the right to go outside whenever they want, but they *choose* not to. They know in their minds that there's always the choice to open that door."

"Ohh? So when you watch a travel program like this, do y'ever feel like going outside, or someplace far away?"

"No, dudette. I never want to go out, but I don't like being cooped up, either."

"Wow. And here I thought you were weird already. You have to be one of the most self-centered guys I've ever met! It's honestly impressive."

"Hey, that's who I am."

"Besides, I should be pretty offended, shouldn't I? You're making it sound like I'm holding you captive in your hospital bed."

Urushihara shut his computer down, the flagging Net connection too much to contend with any longer. "You pretty much are, aren't you?!" he growled at the woman's turned back. "I told you I wanna go home, dudette! But that's fine! I don't care if I can't! I look like *this* now, and—all right, I guess me eavesdropping on you and Chiho Sasaki was bad, for some reason! But I've asked you a million times—who the hell *are* you guys?! What would've been so, like, catastrophic for me to listen in on?!"

"Mmm, I already told you, didn't I? I'm the daughter of Binah, and my aunt Mikitty is kind of the same thing as Alas Ramus. And, Urushihara, what you heard or didn't hear doesn't really matter, all right?"

"I dunno about you, lady, but apart from looking more or less like human females, I really don't think Alas Ramus and our landlord are the same at all!"

"Hmmm? And what makes us so different, may I ask?"

"Daaaaahhhhhhhhhhhhhhhh?!!"

The door opened right as Urushihara was harping on Amane, making him literally leap out of bed.

"Um, are…are you all right, Urushihara?"

He had fallen to the floor, fully clearing the bed's side rails. Amane tried to prop him up, but he clung to her instead, his body erupting into spasms.

"You, you, you didn't say *she'd* show up today!!"

"Oh, did I forget to mention it?"

"Nobody told *me*, dude!!"

"Er, Amane…"

"No! No, I definitely told him! I'm pretty certain that I did! About three days ago!"

The stentorian voice belonged to Miki Shiba. The tone of it put Amane into self-defense mode as she dragged Urushihara back into bed.

"Ah. Well, perhaps you muttered it under your breath while discussing some other subject, and he missed it. How are you feeling, Urushihara?"

"Um… Good? Until you showed up," he managed to gather enough breath to reply. His eyes were unfocused, unable to look directly at Shiba. "Y'know, I used to think it was rude of 'em, but I think I know why Maou and Ashiya said they couldn't look you in the eye. Like, I learned the *hard* way, dude."

"I will take that as a compliment of my womanly charms, thank you."

"Ooof..."

Nothing ever seemed to faze Shiba. To Urushihara, it was no longer any joke. The first time he set eyes upon her photograph, he assumed his demon cohorts were just grossed out by their landlord, this corpulent woman with a penchant for wild clothing and wilder behavior. But when he laid eyes upon the real thing, "grossed out" didn't begin to describe it. Actual changes occurred to his body. Dizziness, and palpitations—but something even beyond that. It felt like simply being in the same room with her was making his most vital strengths stream out of him.

"Well, everyone should be here shortly, so I thought I should alert you first."

"Everyone...?"

"Indeed. Maou, and everyone."

"Whoa! They're back here?!"

His eyes shot open. Then he sneered at Amane next to him.

"Ummm..."

Amane averted her own eyes, attempting to escape from Urushihara's gaze. She seemed one step away from sticking her fingers in her ears and saying, "La-la-la, can't hear you..."

"Regardless," Shiba continued, "once we are all together, I'll have a few things to say to you all. About the Sephirah, and Sephirot, and also about your current state, Urushihara."

"My..."

Urushihara shifted his gaze from Amane and climbed out of bed. He looked at the mirror above the washbasin in one corner of the room and winced.

"Yeah, they're probably gonna be pretty freaked out, fellas... Urp."

As he bemoaned his looks once more, a light wave of nausea crossed his stomach.

✳

Maou, Chiho, Emi, Alas Ramus, Ashiya, Suzuno, Emeralda, Acieth, and Nord all filed out of the three taxis Shiba had hailed for them. Chiho and Maou looked up at the appointed site. Then they turned to each other.

"This is it?"

"Yeah..."

They seemed just as surprised as Emi, Ashiya, and Suzuno behind them.

"Is this...a coincidence?" Emi asked.

"I sincerely hope so."

"No, but is there any other explanation?"

"What is the matterrrr, people?"

"Is this big concern? Or?"

"There something in this hospital?"

Emeralda, Acieth and Nord looked on at the other five, heads cocked in surprise. It took Alas Ramus to finally come out with the truth.

"I been here befo'!"

The building loomed large even in her toddler memory.

Shiba and Amane had taken Urushihara to the Seikai University Hospital in Tokyo, the very place Chiho was admitted after her case of demonic-force poisoning. Chiho, still a bit bewildered, took the lead as they entered this familiar site. Soon, they all stood in front of a certain numbered room.

"Here he is."

"Oh, dear, what will we do if she bills us for this...?"

It was a fairly long distance between the door Chiho pointed out and the adjacent sickroom. A very big room for housing a single patient. No matter how much Shiba assured them not to worry about it, the ominous possibilities made Ashiya sicker with every passing second.

"I have heard," he observed, "of hospital rooms where you have access to television, computers, cell phones, even personal showers."

"Damn. That's better than our place."

Maou and Ashiya exchanged nervous looks before drumming up their resolve and knocking on the door.

"Come in."

"Nhg..."

They heard Shiba's voice on the other side—and it only made them feel sicker. "Will you just open it?" Emi whined. They did, although they needed another deep breath first.

The room was brightly lit by the outside sun. It contained a bed, larger than the one Chiho had been assigned, and the moment they saw the peeved-looking person sitting on it, everyone but Nord froze in place.

"...Dude, what's with *that* reaction?" Urushihara muttered, seeing the exact response he had expected from Maou and the others.

"Oh, no, um..." Maou stammered, looking toward Ashiya for support.

"What in the...?" Ashiya chimed in, similarly unable to offer a complete thought.

"Is this a joke?" Suzuno turned to Emi. "Is Lucifer making light of us again?"

Emi shook her head. "Kind of a long way to go for a joke, isn't it?"

"Indeed," Emeralda added, hand against her chin, "this is not quiiite the Lucifer I am familiarrr with..."

"Wuss' wrong, Lushiferr?" Alas Ramus asked as Acieth gave a look of supreme discomfort to Urushihara.

"Yes. Rough joke, yes."

Urushihara stared back at Acieth, just as frustrated about the rough treatment.

"You think I'd come up with a joke like this by myself?"

"So, what, then? Because this, it very poor taste!"

"Ask our landlord, dude," he replied, motioning toward the calm, composed Shiba by his bed. "It's not like I asked for this!"

"Um, no, but really, Urushihara, what happened?"

Chiho raised a wary finger toward him.

"The...color of your hair...?"

The color of Urushihara's hair had changed to something nobody

was familiar with. Except—they *were* familiar with it, but Urushi-hara had never sported anything like it.

"You think I'm taking this well either, guys? I didn't even do any-thing, and *now* look!"

It was a sheer, almost transparent shade of bluish silver. The exact shade Emilia the Hero sported when wielding her fully powered Better Half—a hue shared with the archangels Sariel or Gabriel. It was something close to that.

"This…is the Great Demon General Lucifer?"

Nord, not being familiar with Urushihara, was the only one who kept a cool head.

"No," Ashiya countered. "This is someone else."

"Dude, Ashiya! Get real, man! And who's that other guy you're with? And Emeralda Etuva, too… What's going on?!"

He had valid complaints, but now didn't seem to be the right time for introductions.

"I believe," Shiba began, "the change in hair color was due to my influence upon him. The human side of his essence must have had a major reaction to my presence. Once he is no longer under my influ-ence, he should return to normal over time."

Whether she meant it as a metaphor or not, Urushihara refused to admit that he and Miki Shiba had any sort of intimate connection that triggered this. Judging by the looks on their faces, Maou and Ashiya were thinking the same thing.

"Regardless," she continued, quieting the room down, "now that you're all here, I think it's time for all of us to really open up to each other. I should be able to explain the full reason behind the hair transformation along the way."

The appeal to calm made Chiho look all the more shocked. "Chiho?" Emi asked, noticing her.

She shook her head in response. "I'm fine."

"You are? You don't look too good…"

"No, it's not that," Chiho said, her eyes brooding as she sized Emi up. "But… I believe in you, okay? And Maou, too."

"Oh? Yeah…"

Emi fell silent, unsure what this meant. But with Chiho not offering anything further, she turned her eyes back to Shiba.

"Now," the landlord said, walking from the bed to the rest of the group, "as you all know, we have a large number of people here from, shall we say, other worlds."

Maou and Ashiya got out of her way, attempting to evade her. She ignored them, tracing a path straight toward Acieth and Emi instead.

"…Yessss?"

Or, to be exact, straight toward Alas Ramus. The child giggled a little, the sensation of Shiba's pudgy fingers caressing her hair perhaps making her ticklish. But the landlord's face in front of hers made Emi nervous—just like Chiho before. She looked at Chiho again, only to find her holding her breath, as if knowing what would come next.

"If you turn your eyes to history, you will find that humans from different worlds interacting with each other is not a rare thing at all. Figuratively, at least, walking to a different nation, or sailing to a different continent, can safely fall under the same umbrella, you could say. What all of you have done is simply the same concept at a larger scale. As I have stated before, the presence of Maou and his friends here in Japan, or Chiho Sasaki in Maou's home of Ente Isla for that matter, is not at all an issue."

But everyone in the room knew what came after that. The atmosphere, and her eyes, told the whole story.

"However… In the case of these two, and these two alone, we must have them return as quickly as we possibly can."

"These two…?" Maou ventured, voice strained by the premonition in his mind.

"Yes," Shiba replied. "Alas Ramus and Acieth Alla. The presence of these two personifications of Yesod, the Sephirah of Ente Isla, poses an extreme danger to the humans that call Ente Isla home."

"Why is that?" a bewildered Suzuno asked. "It is said that Yesod is the jewel that forms the very core of its world, but these two have spent eons as disparate fragments, scattered across the realm, and Ente Isla has never suffered from it."

A while back, when Maou and the others were arguing over whether Alas Ramus should be returned to Yesod guardian Gabriel, Suzuno was the first one to question the authenticity of the Yesod legend. Even if a single precious jewel could form the foundation for an entire world, it had no power to take it away after the fact. If Yesod, which held governance over the moon, were to vanish, would that mean the moon goes, too? Would silver, its associated color, simply disappear? No; that was silly. That was Suzuno's basic argument against returning the child.

"It has never suffered, you say, Ms. Kamazuki?"

"Um..."

But the full bore of Shiba's gaze upon her made Suzuno unable to plead her case further.

"Then what of your powers?"

"M-my powers?" Suzuno looked down at herself.

"Amane and Chiho Sasaki told me themselves. You were gravely wounded after your battle against the demons of another world, and yet you were fully healed after just three days."

"Yes, because of the healing skills derived from my holy force..."

"Then let me ask you, Ms. Kamazuki. Have you ever seen such powers in Japan, or anywhere else on Earth? The power to heal a gash that almost split your body in two...in seventy-two hours? If Chiho Sasaki here sustained a similar injury, I imagine she would require round-the-clock care for a month, just to keep her alive."

"And what of it?"

"You fail to see my point?" Shiba turned back toward Suzuno. "The very 'healing skills' you speak of are part of the problem."

"...Pardon?"

"I am not versed in the history of your world, this Ente Isla. But as far as I have heard from Chiho Sasaki and Nord, it is home to a fairly mature civilization and teems with a great number of people. And yet, powers like those you have are still considered a given in that world. If these children, these Sephirah, were operating correctly in Ente Isla, that could never be the case."

"Um, what do you meeean?" Emeralda nervously asked. "Because as far as I can tell, Lady Shibaaa, you are suggesting that 'holy forrrce' in itself is something that should never even exiiist."

Shiba gave her a casual nod. "And not only that," she continued, sizing up everyone in the room. "The fact that 'holy force' and 'demonic force' are still such overpowering presences across your world hardly strikes me as something beneficial to the Ente Islans."

"What are you talking about?! Are you saying this jewel is balancing the world in some way? That it would fall apart if we lost it?"

"Ms. Kamazuki, you have to listen to me. I do not remember saying that Ente Isla—the world *itself*—is in any danger."

"…What?"

"The only danger that losing the Sephirah and allowing holy and demonic force to continue existing…applies to you. The human race."

"The human…?"

Suzuno was still not fully aware of Shiba's point. She turned to Emi, then Emeralda, then Nord, then to Ashiya and Urushihara and Maou and even Chiho for support. They all gave her confused looks and shakes of the head.

"No matter what state its Sephirah is in, the seas, the skies, the lands, and all the plants and animals of Ente Isla will not be affected at all. Sephirot and the Sephirah only become involved when humans enter the picture. And if Alas Ramus and Acieth Alla do not return to their rightful places, it will spell the extinction of the human race from Ente Isla, in the not-too-distant future."

Considering the portent of her message, the way she put it so flatly, in her matter-of-fact way, made it a little hard to grasp for the Ente Islans in the room who'd be the most affected.

"Of course, by the 'future,' I am not talking about tomorrow or the day after that. By the time all of you live out your natural lives, it may seem like the people of Ente Isla have not been affected by anything at all. But once one hundred years pass, or two hundred, I can no longer make any guarantees."

"O-one hundred years?!"

It was such a long time for someone to live. So many changes could take place in that time. But from the perspective of civilized history, it was all too short. Especially among the demons in the room, whose lifespans were measured more in terms of millennia than centuries.

"Um, Ms. Shiba," Ashiya hesitantly replied, "it seems preposterous to me that every human on Ente Isla will perish in a mere century..."

Shiba gave him a slight nod. "I imagine so, yes. But with the current state of things, it is an open question whether it could last five... more like three centuries, if that. If a giant meteor were to hit the planet, that would be another story, but even if there was no natural disaster like that...as long as people still use holy and demonic force like this, the humans of Ente Isla have no future. Slowly but surely, their numbers will dwindle, and then they will perish, unable to do anything to halt it."

"What do you mean by that?" Emi boldly asked, as the rest of them were left spellbound by Shiba's doomsday scenario. "I'm not just going to smile and hand Alas Ramus back unless I know how her Sephirah and our people are actually connected. She and Acieth are...a treasure to me. To everyone in this room. To them, 'where they were' means the heavens above Ente Isla. The home of a pack of angels who think nothing of their fates, or the fates of anyone else on our planet. I can't let these girls go back there."

"Ah, yes, about the angels. That man, Gabriel, woke up the other day."

"Gabriel did?"

"Yes. And he had some rather distressing news." Shiba breathed out a light sigh. "He attempted to flee back to heaven the moment he awoke. It happened so suddenly that I almost lost hold of him... but thanks to what, for him, was rather unhappy news, he failed to escape."

"Unhappy news?"

Maou and Ashiya eyed each other. Neither could think of anything unhappier than being in Shiba's house, under her personal care, although they both thought it best not to mention that.

"He said that the 'heaven' of Ente Isla—the place that Alas Ramus and Acieth need to return to—has been closed off. It no longer accepts any outside contact, and no Gate can reach it at present. Perhaps *they* have given up on these children so much that they've cut them out of the picture."

"Closed off...? Come to think of it, something has been bothering me a little." Emi turned toward Maou. "Devil King?"

"Hmm?"

"Where are the demon realms?"

"...Uh?" he replied, as if being asked the stupidest question of his life. "Are you serious?"

"What? Of course I am." Emi sullenly glared at him. "Is it under Ente Isla, like how the typical heaven-and-hell diagram works? Or is it a different planet, like Earth...?"

"Don't be stupid. You really didn't know?"

Maou gave Ashiya and Urushihara a perplexed look. They both shrugged.

"Well, admittedly, my liege, I do not believe we ever spelled out the location to anyone."

"Yeah, not like anyone asked!"

"Huh. Guess not. Well, not that it matters, but...it's the moon."

"What?" Emi gasped. Chiho, next to her, balled up her fists a little, without anyone noticing.

"Whaddaya mean, what? I said, the moon. The red one you can see from Ente Isla? That's where the demon realms are."

"The... The moon?!" Suzuno shouted. "Then..."

"Yeah, heaven's on the blue one," Urushihara blurted out.

"Another world, indeed!" Shiba remarked as she opened the curtains blocking the window. Light from outside filled the room, revealing a view of the tall buildings around Seikai University Hospital, thrusting into the skies around Yoyogi.

"Neither the Earth, nor Ente Isla, nor the realm where one may find the tree of Sephirot, are located in any alternate dimension or timeline."

She spread an arm toward the sunny view, taking in the skies of Tokyo.

"Earth and Ente Isla are simply two planets floating in space, connected by the skies between them, brimming with humanity."

"…They are…?"

Emi sighed. It was a thought that had vaguely existed in her mind ever since she arrived in Japan. She hadn't gone as far as Acieth did, visiting observatories and studying amateur astronomy and so on, but she had learned well enough that the Earth was just one of many planets spinning in space. The fact the Earth was round, along with things like the law of gravity, she naturally picked up on from TV, movies, and the Internet.

But what about her own world? It had people who looked just the same as those here, a perfectly breathable atmosphere, and thousands of stars in the night sky. It didn't take her long to conclude that Ente Isla was another round planet, just like Earth.

Not even this, however, prepared her to think that heaven, and the demon realms, were on Ente Isla's moons. The news didn't particularly change things around her. It took the vague concept of "another world" and gave it a concrete definition, but it didn't mean she'd be taking a train or plane between Earth and Ente Isla anytime soon.

On the other hand, the news that not even a Gate could get one inside heaven almost seemed like good news to her, Gabriel's perspective notwithstanding. The heavens had done nothing but consistently meddle with her and Alas Ramus, and now they had excused themselves from the party. But Shiba remained grim.

"In order for the Sephirah to function properly, all of them must be together. By what Acieth tells me, Yesod, and Yesod alone, has been separated from the rest of the Sephirah for centuries. I could not say what kind of ill effect this has had on them."

"The other Sephirah…"

Ashiya's whisper reminded Maou of Erone, the personification of the Sephirah known as Gevurah. He was serving the heavens, it seemed, but between Acieth and the guardian angel Camael who was with him, this was no standard master-and-servant relationship. Ashiya was the only one to make contact with him during the battle in Efzahan, and now his arms were crossed before Shiba.

"This 'ill effect' you speak of...?"

"I cannot say. The effect of Yesod's absence has already manifested itself in the form of 'holy magic,' but I cannot provide any more guidance than that unless I see for myself. What I *can* see, however, is that there is nothing we can do about it. I will be forced to leave it all up to you instead."

"You can't do anything...?"

Maou winced. All that exposition, and then Shiba just dropped everything into their own laps.

"Well, whaddaya want?" Amane said, stepping in. "Aunt Mikitty is the Sephirah of Earth. She's only supposed to be using her powers for people over here."

"The Sephirah...?" Maou said, voice betraying a twinge of disbelief. "Is it true, by the way? Like, you're the same as Alas Ramus and Acieth?"

Shiba casually nodded at him. "I am not part of Yesod myself, and there may be some slight differences in my role from other Sephirah, but..."

"Then may I ask," Suzuno said, "which Sephirah you are?"

If she knew which of the ten Sephirah Shiba had been born from, there would be no easier way to verify this story. But Shiba's reply was literally one step beyond what she anticipated.

"I am the eleventh Sephirah."

"...Eleventh?"

Suzuno blinked. This number wasn't in her knowledge. As the scriptures put it, there were ten Sephirah forming the cores of worlds.

"...I am not aware of an eleventh. That, if anything, could be the illest wind of all affecting Ente Isla. I believe Acieth was unaware of this, as well."

"I don't know what is not there," Acieth indifferently replied.

But someone else in the room reacted to the number in quite a different way.

"The eleventh Sephirah... Huh. I think someone told me about that..."

"Urushihara?"

"Oh, yeah, I remember," he said, as if recalling what he had for dinner last night. "Satan told me."

"Huh? Me?" Maou stammered. "Did I ever talk to you about that? And not to Camio or someone?"

The Devil King had himself only learned the Sephirah tale from Camio, his current Devil Regent, and he couldn't remember how long ago it had happened. He was later able to supplant this information with Church scripture he seized during the Ente Isla invasion, but that was purely for his own curiosity; he didn't recall using it for anything, or telling anyone else about it.

That's why it was no surprise when Urushihara shook his head and hands at once.

"No, dude, I'm not talking about you. It was..."

"""Satan, the ancient Devil Overlord."""

Three people said it in unison. One was Urushihara, of course. The other, oddly enough, was Acieth. And the third was the most unlikely of all.

"Chiho?"

Emi and the rest all looked at her, mouths agape. Even Urushihara and Acieth were caught off guard.

"Wha—?"

"Chiho?"

"Wait, why do *you* know, Chiho Sasaki? Did you say something to her, Maou?"

"No," Maou said, shaking his head at his shocked audience. He, along with Shiba and Amane, closely studied Chiho, who was not caught up in the initial wave of surprise.

"So why does Chiho Sasaki know that phrase? 'Ancient Devil Overlord' and all?"

"I am more curious about Acieth myself," Ashiya stated, "but Ms. Sasaki, where did you hear about such a person?"

Chiho looked at Ashiya, serious-faced.

"M-Ms. Sasaki?"

Something looked strange about her to him. As a non–Ente Islan, Chiho hadn't figured much in this conversation so far, simply listening intently to the proceedings. But now her actions seemed... out of place. Her face was serious, but also empty, like nothing was behind her eyes—and yet, she also had an odd air of self-assured composure.

"I know all about him," she replied, words almost disappearing into the air before reaching their ears. "Satan, the ancient Devil Overlord."

Amane's entire body tensed up.

"Aunt Mikitty, is that...?"

"I would imagine so," Shiba replied, wholly unaffected.

"...Chi! What do you know?!"

Maou's shout attracted the eyes of everyone in the room. He raised a right hand to stop Shiba and the nervous Amane from interrupting further.

"Keep quiet a sec. This has happened before," he said, motioning at the rest of the room to stay where they were. "You... You've got something to tell us, don't you?"

"Yes," came Chiho's reply, her voice now unfathomable to him.

""""...!"""" Emi, Ashiya, and Suzuno visibly reared back, still just barely recovered from Maou's outburst of a moment ago.

"""""...""""""

Then they noticed Maou's left hand move a little. They each eyed the other, out of eyeshot of Chiho.

"...Rrh?"

"Pop? What is it?" the sharp-eyed Acieth asked, noticing Nord let a wincing groan out from his throat.

"N-no, I... I just had a bit of a dizzy spell. I'm fine..."

Maou gave him a quick glance before returning to the business at hand. "Tell me," he asked. "What do you know?"

Chiho, still not noticing Emi, Ashiya, or Suzuno, slowly opened her mouth.

"The eleventh Sephirah was once known as the 'Devil Overlord,' the an—"

"Get her!!"

The warm, almost-lilting voice was cut short by Maou's suddenly barked order. The trio he directed his orders to sprang into action. Immediately, Ashiya took position by the double doors in front of the closet, Suzuno by the sliding door to the unit bath, and Emi close to the other sliding door leading to the hospital hallway. All at once, they flung the doors wide open.

""Agh!!""

There were two short screams on top of each other. Emi wound up being the lucky winner. Beyond her door, there stood a scared-looking nurse, perhaps startled by the hospital-room door being rattled open so quickly without warning. That was one scream. The other was from Chiho.

"Grab her, Emi!!"

"Ahh!!"

"N... Huhh?"

Emi had no need for Maou's instructions. She grabbed the nurse by the collar and pulled her inside the room, almost quickly enough to give her whiplash. As Acieth and Nord watched from behind in disbelief, Chiho let out a confused groan, as if waking up from a dream.

"Wh-wh-what are you *doing*?!" the nurse shrieked, half-panicking at these visitors' bizarre behavior. Or so it must have looked to the other observers. But Emi refused to release the nurse's collar, and Ashiya and Suzuno quickly stationed themselves by the door and window, sealing off all routes of escape.

"What is the meaning of this? I'm calling for security!"

"Go ahead," Maou retorted, slowly walking up to her, "if you can."

Dressed in a sensible, clean-looking light blue gown, the nurse—probably in her late twenties—attempted to claw her way out of Emi's grasp.

"I've got a light smoke screen of demonic force covering the room," Maou said—and with that, she stopped. "You see how that dude over there's already reeling from it. No normal human being could come in here and *not* start to feel dizzy and faint. Guess you're pretty strong against it, huh?"

"...Ah."

"That wasn't the same kind of canned message you gave us last time. Chi and I were having a real *conversation* just now. I knew you were pretty close by, but this is just ridiculous."

"..."

The nurse, still detained by Emi's iron grip, relented at Maou's voice. Her eyes silently scanned the people assembled in the room.

"...Whoa! Wait, what? Yusa, what're you doing to her?!"

Chiho's obvious question interrupted the tension. As if on cue, it made the nurse relax her body, her head hung down in shame.

"...Well," she said, suddenly sounding very different, "I sure screwed this one up..."

"I'm gonna punch you," a clearly annoyed Maou said, raising a fist.

"I don't remember teaching you it was okay to hit a woman."

"You know I'm the Devil King now, don't you? That's what I do. Plus, hey, that's why they call it 'equal rights,' okay?"

"I don't think this is what they meant..."

"Your Demonic Highness, did this woman...possess Ms. Sasaki?"

"Huh? Me?"

Chiho blinked at Ashiya's question as Maou nodded.

"Who is this freak?" Emi asked, harried. "Because you're acting like she was mind-controlling Chiho or something, and you even know who she is."

She gave the nurse in her arms another look. She was about as tall as her, wearing a green surgical mask, her hair tied back with a number of pins during her on-duty hours. At a glance, she looked like any other Japanese woman. Emi didn't know her.

But:

"Emi?"

"What?"

"I know she's acting like a total ass, but you probably better not call her 'that freak.'"

"Huh?"

"Hey," Maou called out next to the confused Emi, "you want me to tell her? 'Cause I will if you don't say something."

"...Oh, well."

At that moment, the nurse's voice made a complete transformation. It had the desired effect.

"!!"

Nord, still queasy at the light miasma of demonic force surrounding him, shot back to attention.

"No..."

The nurse looked toward him sadly...

"Ah!"

...and suddenly began to emit light from her entire body.

"Emi, hang on to her! Ashiya, Suzuno, keep her in the room!"

"Wh-wha—?! What's...?!"

"Yes, my—"

"Nnh!"

"I'm going nowhere," came a voice from the light, cutting all three of them off.

"—?!" Emi gasped.

Nord managed another "What?!!" of shock.

Emeralda pointed at her and went "Ahhh...!!"

And in the midst of it all, Alas Ramus simply looked up and said, "That... Mommy...?"

The flowing bluish-silver hair and crimson eyes were a match for Gabriel's, an indicator she was an angel from heaven. But among this audience, that was just a minor detail. Everyone was more fixated on her other features.

"...Sorry," the beautiful angel said, smiling awkwardly while Emi still held her in the air by her collar. "Guess I could've handled that better."

Maou rolled his eyes. "Just the kind of pain in the ass we needed at a time like this," he said, even as the sight brought back a few fond memories. "But I hope you're ready for this. We're not gonna feed you 'til you tell us everything you know. Because I think we've all had enough of you using and abusing us."

"Okay... I know—*upph*!"

She answered Maou's annoyed but still gentle voice with a muffled groan that made her seem not quite as divine as before. Emi used the hand that wasn't holding her by the scruff to give her a slap on the cheek.

"..."

"Um...hey, Emi?"

"E-Emilia! Wait! She's..."

Maou's and Nord's attempts to dissuade Emi were greeted with a sneer more sinister than any they had seen before.

"..."

""Eep!!"" It made both the leader of all demons and her own father visibly whimper.

"Um, uh, uh, hey..."

Meanwhile, the slappee looked blankly at Emi, unsure what had just happened.

"Listen, Emi—*bweh*!"

The attempt at conversation was interrupted with another slap.

"Keep your mouth closed."

"Um, that, wait just a—*pwff*!!"

"I'm not waiting any longer."

"P-please! I promise I'll tell you every*thnnh*!"

"Don't expect to make me forgive you that easily."

"U-uh, um, please, listen to—*fwwh*!"

"I'm listening. But once I'm done listening, it's gonna be even worse for you. That's about what you did to me, so..."

"L-listen, I really feel bad about that! I do! You can do whatever you want to me afterward, so please, let me go! And stop slapping me*hnnh*!"

The dry cracks that came every few words echoed across the room, as the angel's teary-eyed pleading was greeted by a pair of eyes turned down to absolute zero.

"Emi! Emi! That's too much! That's too much, okay? She won't be able to talk! She's looking like some kid in a cartoon with a toothache!"

"Emiliaaa! Please, calm dowwwn!"

"Yusa! Don't do that! Don't do any more of that!"

"Keep eyes away from her, okay, big sis?"

"What're...? What're my mommies doing...?"

"E-Emilia, Emilia! Please, hold it back for now! Please! This is your father asking you to!"

Nord was trying to get a grip on Emi's arm as her friends rose to stop the onslaught and Acieth rose to shield Alas Ramus from the sordid display.

"Owwwww..."

By the time the violence ended, the face of the beautiful angel was looking like a mix between a Napoleon fish and a giant trevally.

"...nh...!"

The glassy-eyed Emi was still trying to swing her left hand around, stopped only by the combined efforts of Emeralda and Chiho.

"Look," Maou said, leaving the pair to their impromptu guard duty, "I'm not gonna do anything to you, so can you just tell us everything, from start to end, no excuses. 'Cause if you don't, I'm not too sure we can protect you from that girl right now, okay? She might even kill you."

"All right..."

The teary agreement, as she let Nord support her weight, was in a quiet voice that was far thinner, and more forlorn, than Maou remembered. He sighed and slumped his shoulders.

"You're just as indecipherable as you were then, you know that?"

He recalled the vague memory he had of his young-demon days, somewhere in the back of his mind—a time when he all but gave up on life, never dreaming that he would someday rule over every demon that walked the realm.

"It's been a while, huh, Laila?"

The little demon and beautiful angel who met atop that red moon in the sky were now united on a new, much bluer planet.

THE AUTHOR, THE AFTERWORD, AND YOU!

Plunging into a new environment can always make a person nervous. In academics, maybe it's changing classes or schools, or graduating to a new grade, or going to part-time jobs or after-school learning centers. When you're grown up, it could involve changing jobs, departments, or addresses.

Every time you find yourself in a new environment, it's easy to start worrying over the unknowns ahead, losing sleep over it. I imagine everyone's experienced that at one point or another. Before *The Devil is a Part-Timer!* saw the light of day, I got a phone call saying I was one of the finalists in the Dengeki Novel Prize. I was asked to report to the editorial office in a few days, and during that tiny interval, I, Wagahara, spent every waking moment fretting over nothing, wondering what would happen next. I'd make careless errors at work that I'd never normally commit, and I'd find myself feeling queasy at times.

I'll never forget the first day I reported to their office. I arrived at the building a good twenty minutes before my appointment, and as I tried to kill the time, I wound up trotting to the public bathroom in the nearby Shinjuku Central Park, unloading everything I had at full throttle in there, no less than four times in fifteen minutes.

The days between my first visit and the release of *Devil*'s first volume meant a return to constant fretting. Being asked to write a sequel set it off again, and I never stopped worrying until *that* one was on the shelves. I've gone through the process over and over again—and before I knew it, *The Devil is a Part-Timer!* now wraps up its eleventh volume.

Whenever I write a new story, I sometimes get anxious over whether this is still important to me—whether I've forgotten the emotions I brought with me at first. But if we're here rapping at each other again, I suppose that means I haven't—which is good.

This volume is set to be released in May of 2014 in Japan. They say spring is a time for new encounters (as well as a time when students nationwide contract a killer case of senioritis), and I suppose one's ability to get used to a new situation (or not) is a kind of watershed in their lives.

In Volume 11, we see the characters expressing frustration over the brand-new environment they're thrust into, fretting over how to deal with it, and ultimately deciding to worry over how to put food on the table tomorrow instead of obsessing over things they can't even see. It's a turning point, one where a few of the mysteries accompanying the story began to unshroud themselves. I hope you enjoyed the eleventh volume, and I hope I'll see you again in the next one.

Until then!